TO THE DEATH!

When Captain Nathan Kelso has a falling-out with his commanding officer, Major Matthew Hackett, Company 'C' is unofficially disbanded — but not for long, with broncos and Apaches raising hell throughout the territory. Then a patrol under a green lieutenant is all but wiped out, and an incident involving two rabid coyotes results in Hackett being badly injured. When things go from bad to worse, Kelso must lead his men into the Santa Rita Mountains on a do-or-die mission that will see him and Company 'C' fighting — to the death!

BRENT TOWNS

TO THE DEATH!

Complete and Unabridged

LINFORD
Leicester

First published in Great Britain in 2017 by
Bookends
London

First Linford Edition
published 2018
by arrangement with
Kindle
London

A catalogue record for this book is available
from the British Library.

ISBN 978–1–4448–3917–3

Published by
F. A. Thorpe (Publishing)
Anstey, Leicestershire

Set by Words & Graphics Ltd.
Anstey, Leicestershire
Printed and bound in Great Britain by
T. J. International Ltd., Padstow, Cornwall

This book is printed on acid-free paper

This one is for Sam and Jacob

'All the tribes tell the same story. They are surrounded on all sides, the game is destroyed or driven away; they are left to starve, and there remains but one thing for them to do — fight while they can.'
— George Crook.

'When I was young I walked all over this country, east and west, and saw no other people than the Apaches. After many summers I walked again and found another race of people had come to take it. How is it?'
— Cochise.

'I should never have surrendered. I should have fought until I was the last man alive.'
— Geronimo.

'Ride hard, fight harder.'
— Captain Nathan Kelso,
Company 'C'.

The man had been dead for two days, and putrefaction had been swift to set in.

Lew Eden, a thirty-five-year-old Seminole-Negro scout who worked out of Fort Whitethorn, Arizona Territory, had been tracking the bronco Apaches who'd killed him for the past week now, and was still no closer to running them to ground. In fact, this was the closest he'd come to them so far.

Two days.

Two damned days.

He sighed and pushed his high-crowned hat back to reveal short black hair. He wore a brown bib shirt and black jeans tucked into high black boots, and about his waist was buckled a thick shell belt with every loop full. Tucked behind it was a double-action 1878, .41 caliber revolver. On the opposite side, a well-honed, stone-headed hatchet rested in a beaded sheath.

Lew's father had been a slave, his mother a Seminole Indian. Before working at Whitethorn, he'd served with the Seminole-Negro Scouts on the plains of Texas, where he'd fought various tribes including Comanche and Cheyenne. He'd even served in the Sioux war after '75.

But here in the desert, fighting Apaches was a whole different war. Apaches were highly skilled at surviving in and using the desert to their full advantage. It was said — with some justification — that an Apache could ride right past and you'd never even know he was there if that's the way he wanted it. They traveled light and knew where all the waterholes were. They adapted and overcame.

To beat the Apache, you had to out-Apache him. That's why the outfit to which he had been assigned, Company 'C', had been formed. Travel light and hit hard, just like the Indians themselves. It had been the brainchild of his friend, Captain Nathan Kelso, and after some resistance, had been sanctioned by General George Crook himself.

Although their first mission had been a success, no one had yet seen fit to give them something else to handle. Lew suspected that had something to do with the mutual dislike between Kelso and his commanding officer, Major Matthew Hackett. Then again, maybe it was the fact that Kelso had issues with the bottle.

Whichever, it had seen Company 'C' unofficially disbanded and the men returned to their original units.

That was the reason Lew now found himself at Willow Springs, surrounded by a harsh landscape of sand, rock, cholla, barrel cactus, and ocotillo, in searing heat, beside an empty water-hole, with a dead man whose name, in life, had been Soapy Smith. Soapy had been a prospector who'd roamed the southern regions of Arizona, looking to strike it rich, for years. He never had, of course, and now he never would. Two Apache arrows sticking from his chest and a missing scalp guaranteed that.

The bronco Apaches Lew was tracking were like ghosts of the desert, and their leader, a chief named Beshe, was as brutal as they came. For some reason, the small war band, numbering some fifteen braves in strength, had left their stronghold in the Mogollon Range and cut a bloody swathe through Arizona.

A squawk drew Lew's attention and he cast a glance fifty yards left, to where buzzards feasted on the remains of Smith's mule. They waddled around the carcass, so stuffed with meat that they could barely move, let alone fly.

On a saguaro-covered ridge to the east, Lew caught the flash of sunlight reflecting from some kind of polished surface. He quickly turned to glance at a large hill to the west and was just in time to see another flash answer the first. Then movement caught his eye and an Apache sitting atop a wiry mustang appeared. He was quickly joined by another, and yet one more.

'Just the three of you?' Lew murmured in his deep, baritone voice.

He turned back to the east and found himself staring at another three. Slowly he walked across to his ground-hitched pinto. He picked up the reins and climbed into the saddle. The Apaches still sat unmoving on both sides. Stocky men, they didn't even match Lew's modest five feet ten.

The dust cloud to the north was the next thing to draw his attention. He realized then that they were going to try forcing him south, further into the desert, away from Whitethorn and the remote possibility of any help.

Lew thought. *Hell with that.*

He leaned forward, drew the cavalry issue, single-shot .45/.70 Springfield and set it across his lap. He looked toward the sun. Maybe three hours of daylight left, he decided. He patted his pinto on the neck and talked to it in a soothing voice. Then he pointed it south and rode off. Before he'd traveled thirty yards, he had the pinto moving fluidly at a steady pace.

When he looked back, he saw that the Apaches on both sides were coming down onto the flat, dragging a large rooster tail of dust behind them. They would soon join up with the rest of the broncos and harry him until he was captured or killed.

The only problem was, they'd never come across a man quite like Lew Eden.

★   ★   ★

Captain Nathan Kelso stood before his commanding officer, bleary-eyed and smelling like a whiskey still. He wasn't sure what felt worse at six in the morning — his pounding head, or the hard-edged voice of Major Matthew Hackett.

'Did you hear me, Kelso?' snapped

the major. 'I asked you where the hell that scout of yours has gotten to?'

Kelso's hazel-green eyes were blood-shot and his curly blue-black hair was unkempt from where Sergeant Mordecai Shannon had taken great pleasure in rousing him from sleep. A moderately-built man, he straightened to his full six feet and said, 'If I remember rightly, sir, he isn't my scout anymore.'

'Don't split hairs,' Hackett snapped, blue eyes flaring.

'No, sir.'

Hackett's office was small but tidy. The colonial stove in one corner faced the major's heavy desk in the other. Hackett stood up and came around to the front of his desk, revealing a tunic that struggled to accommodate his thickening waist. 'I'll ask again,' he said. 'Where is Eden? He's been gone over a week. It was my understanding that he was undertaking a simple scouting mission, and yet there is still no sign of him. Meanwhile, reports are still coming in about the blasted Apaches he's supposed to be finding.'

'I'm sure he has his reasons, sir,' Kelso answered. He hesitated briefly, then added, 'I could always take Company 'C' out on patrol, with orders to find him. We might even be able to flush those broncos out while we're at it.'

Hackett snorted derisively. 'Send the lieutenant in on your way out,' he replied. 'Dismiss.'

Kelso considered saying more but almost immediately decided against it. Instead, he spun on his heel, caught himself as he lost balance momentarily, then marched from the room, leaving the door open. As he passed through the outer office, he growled to Lieutenant Miller, 'He wants to see you,' and kept going.

Fort Whitethorn was a standard military outpost with adobe buildings surrounded by a low, whitewashed stone wall. Along the west wall stood an infirmary, guardhouse, stables, and corral. The eastern wall was home to the enlisted men's barracks, kitchen, and mess hall. The commanding officer's, adjutant's, and officers' quarters resided along the north wall, alongside the officers' kitchen and mess, and the married quarters.

Outside the wall lay the town of Ocotillo Creek, whose main street finished at the gates of Fort Whitethorn.

'Are we goin' out, sir?'

Kelso turned and looked at Private Ruben Brady, a lanky, dark-haired man from Texas whom he had chosen to ride with Company 'C'. Kelso shook his head, 'No.'

'I just thought we might've got lucky,' Brady muttered.

Impulsively, Kelso asked, 'Have you seen Lew Eden this morning?'

'No, sir. Haven't seen him for days, now.'

'All right. Carry on, soldier.'

He watched Brady walk off, then raised a trembling hand to his throbbing temple. He felt terrible, and the

9

knowledge that his condition was self-inflicted only made him feel worse. He hated that he had come to rely on the bottle to ease his frustrations, but only had himself to blame. He hadn't started out to become a drunk. He'd joined up because he'd wanted to make a difference. Only it hadn't worked out that way. Instead, he'd found himself posted from one Godforsaken post to another and given few if any jobs that would really make the civilians who'd settled in these remote parts feel any safer.

Loneliness had played its part, too, of course. Long evenings spent alone because he had nothing in common with fellow officers whose only concern was their own personal advancement. Loneliness, and boredom.

And so he had started drinking — not much, at first. Just enough to take the edge off his increasingly disgruntled mood, to help him sleep at night.

In the end, everyone on the post

knew he'd become a drunk except him. The curling of lips whenever he passed a fellow officer, the dark mutterings of enlisted men when they saw him coming . . . God, he'd been so damn slow to realize what had happened! And by the time it *had* happened, it was already too late. He couldn't live without the next drink.

That in itself terrified him. It terrified him so much that he'd decided to do something about it. And for as long as he'd been training and leading Company 'C' — a special unit who travelled light and used the Apache's own guerilla tactics against them — he felt that he had beaten his demons.

But he'd reckoned without Major Hackett.

No matter that George Crook had given his support to Company 'C' — Hackett was determined to run Fort Whitethorn by the book, and fight the Indians in the same, hopeless manner.

And so he had turned back to the booze and lost whatever respect he'd managed to regain.

Even now, he was thinking about the bottle he had stashed away in his bachelor's quarters, how it would temper the anger and disappointment in him. Then he thought again about Hackett and Hackett's refusal to use him and his men.

'Damn you!' he muttered.

A corporal from B Company was passing by and stopped to look at him. He said, 'Beg pardon, cap'n?'

Kelso held up his hand in apology. 'Nothing, Corporal. Carry on.'

Once the corporal was gone, Kelso looked out above the adobe buildings of the fort to the surrounding hills.

'Where are you, Lew?' he murmured. 'Where the *hell* are you?'

★   ★   ★

Thirty miles to the southeast of Fort Whitethorn, Lew Eden found himself looking over another scene of slaughter. For two days, he'd evaded the broncos

12

who'd been on his trail. After he'd left the scene of Soapy Smith's demise, he'd ridden the pinto south and circled to the east, then back north where he stumbled across the scene he was now witnessing from atop a low hill.

The dark smudge of rising smoke stained the clear Arizona sky. Small orange flames licked at the few remaining charred timbers of the burnt out barn. The adobe homestead still stood, although the front door hung from one hinge and its contents had been scattered about outside. To the left of the burning barn, the corral stood empty.

Even from this vantage, Lew could see three bodies lying on the hard-packed earth of the homestead's yard. He knew who they were — Isom Randall and his two sons, Isiah and Luke. He guessed Isom's wife, Laura, would be inside.

Lew let the tired pinto pick its way slowly down the rock and cactus-covered hillside. When the horse reached the bottom, it walked between two large paloverde trees and into the open. He climbed down and checked the three bodies. They had all been shot and scalped. Isom and Luke also had arrows in them.

Lew bent and plucked one of the arrows out of Isom, looked it over, and frowned at it.

The arrow was Mimbreño.

What were the Mimbreños doing this far west?

It seemed as if Arizona was becoming a hotbed for renegade activity.

Isom Randall's wife was indeed inside. Lew found her where the Apaches had left her, stripped naked on the marital bed. She had been brutally violated and her throat slashed. He carried her outside, wrapped in a blanket, and lay her beside her husband and sons.

The family had been killed the day before and the Mimbreños had relieved the homestead of supplies and what few horses they had. They'd taken all weapons and ammunition, too.

Finding a shovel, Lew buried the family under one of the large paloverde trees. Once his somber task was complete, he scouted the area surrounding the homestead. The Mimbreños had come out of a dry creek bed to the north. He figured there must have been at least forty of them, maybe more. They'd taken the Randalls by surprise during their morning chores; Isom and his folks hadn't stood a chance.

Now Lew's priority was to report back to Whitethorn. They needed to know what was happening before the whole of southern Arizona went up in flames.

⋆   ⋆   ⋆

'Damn that girl!' Hackett's furious voice rang throughout his office after he finished reading the note in his hand. 'Headstrong just like her mother was.'

He read it again and called to the

15

outer office, 'Lieutenant!'

Hackett's adjutant, Crispin Miller, hurried into the room. 'Sir?'

'It would seem that my daughter will be joining us here at the fort,' Hackett announced.

Miller's eyebrows shot up, 'Amelia, sir? When?'

'Two days from now.'

'She hasn't given you much notice, major.'

'No, she hasn't,' agreed Hackett. 'She knows I would have forbidden her from coming at all, with things as they are with the Apaches! This way, she hasn't given me the chance!' He shook his head. 'Have one of the married women set her up in my spare room. And ask her nicely if she would tidy the place up. A single man's home out here is no place for a young lady like Amelia.'

'Yes, sir. I'll see to it.'

The door closed behind Miller, and Hackett walked over to the window that overlooked the parade ground. From there he could also see the entrance to the fort and out along Ocotillo Creek's main street.

'Damn it,' he cursed once more. 'This is no place for her.'

He was still thinking that when he saw the rider approaching the fort's main gate, riding slowly, and rocking to match his horse's smooth stride.

'Miller!'

Again, the door opened. 'Sir?'

'Get Kelso,' he snapped. 'His damned scout's back.'

2

Lew said, 'You got a problem, Major.'

Hackett's eyes sparked briefly as he looked up at the dust-covered scout. 'You're right,' he agreed. 'I sent you to scout for Beshe's bronco Apaches and you disappeared off the face of the earth for the better part of a week and a half.'

'You didn't ask me how long I expected to take,' Lew replied easily. 'An' there was no way of tellin'. But that's the difference 'twixt you and the Apaches, I reckon. White men got no patience.'

'The army pays you to follow orders, Eden, not to smart-mouth me. I expected you back after four days.'

'Then you should have said so. My orders were to find the broncos that's causin' all the trouble. I did that and more.'

Eyes flaring, Hackett was about to continue when Kelso cut him off. 'Maybe we should hear what Lew has to say before you go passing judgment . . . sir.'

Hackett gave Kelso an angry stare before he nodded abruptly. 'All right, captain.' He shifted his gaze to the scout. 'Proceed.'

Lew threw the Mimbreño arrow onto Hackett's desk. 'Like I said — you got a problem.' He went over to the wall where a rough map of the surrounding area was pinned. He stabbed a thick finger at it and said in his baritone voice, 'Two days ago, I found Beshe and his broncos here. Or rather, they found me.'

Kelso saw that Lew had indicated a place known as Willow Springs.

'They forced me to run south, away from any kind of help. I managed to circle back, though, and lost them after two days. That was . . . here.'

Again, his finger tapped the map indicating a position some thirty miles southeast.

19

'Isn't there a homestead in that area?' Hackett asked.

'Not anymore,' said Lew. 'That's where I found that arrow early this morning. The Randalls were attacked and slaughtered yesterday. The menfolk straight up. Mrs. Randall wasn't so lucky.'

Hackett picked up the arrow and examined it. He stared at it dumbly, having no idea what he was really supposed to be looking at. He handed it off to Kelso, who gave it a closer examination, despite the faint tremor in his hands.

'Is this right, Lew?' he asked after a moment.

'Yes, cap'n.'

'A little outta their territory, aren't they?'

'I thought so, too,' Lew agreed. 'But then, so are Beshe and his warriors.'

'True.'

Hackett cleared his throat. 'Would someone like to tell me what's so special about that arrow?'

'The arrow is Mimbreño,' Kelso explained. 'By rights, the Mimbreños should be miles from here.'

'How strong a war party, Mr. Eden?' Hackett asked.

'Forty or so, maybe more.'

'Do you have any idea who they are?'

'Some.'

'Well?'

'I think it is a band led by Bodaway.'

'Who?'

'Roughly, the name translates to Firemaker, sir,' Kelso put in. 'It makes sense. He's a Mimbreño chief. He's also the grandson of Baishan, better known as Cuchillo Negro. I think you had better inform General Crook, sir.'

Hackett thought for a moment, ignoring the suggestion. 'What else, Mr. Eden?'

'Their tracks headed east, but given the time frame between then and now, they could be just about anywheres.'

Hackett cursed. 'Of all the damned times to visit,' he muttered.

'Beg pardon, sir?' said Kelso.

'My daughter is coming in on the stage the day after tomorrow. As you can see, the timing couldn't be more inconvenient.'

'Do you want me to take Company 'C' out to track them down, sir?' Kelso asked. 'We can be gone by noon.'

Hackett looked at Kelso and shook his head. 'No, captain. I have something *else* in mind for you.'

Lew saw the disappointment on Kelso's face and wondered how many times a man could be knocked down before he finally stayed down.

The major turned to Lew and said, 'Thank you, Mr. Eden, that will be all. On your way out, find Lieutenant Reardon for me. He's skulking about out there somewhere. When you do, tell him I want to see him.'

Once the scout had gone, Kelso opened his mouth to speak, but his commanding officer cut him off.

'Don't start, captain,' he snapped. 'I noticed the state you were in this morning. I also know that Sergeant

Shannon had to drag you out of bed when you should've already been seeing to other duties. If I ever catch you drinking on duty, or if I suspect your drinking is liable to put a single man under my command in danger, I'll have you drummed out of this man's army so fast your head will spin.'

A heavy silence settled between them.

A few moments later the door opened and Reardon entered. 'You wanted to see me, major?'

Reardon was a rail-thin twenty-two-year-old with blond hair and blue eyes. He would have looked more at home in some gentleman's club back east than he did out in the Arizona desert.

'You wanted to get some field experience, lieutenant,' said Hackett. 'Well, here's your chance. I want you to assemble a detail from Company 'A'. Twenty-five men should do. Take Seamus Murphy with you as your sergeant. Draw sufficient supplies and ammunition to last for two weeks.'

23

Reardon was unable to conceal his excitement. 'Yes, sir!' Then: 'Umm, what is it you want me to do exactly, sir?'

Hackett crossed to the map. Guessing what was coming, Kelso said, 'With respect, sir, Lieutenant Reardon has had no experience with something like this. Let me take . . .'

'No!' Hackett snapped. 'I've already told you, you and your command are going to be doing something else. Lieutenant, we have some troublesome Apaches out there somewhere. Your orders are to run them to ground and take prisoner any you are not forced to kill.'

'At least let Lew Eden go along with him, sir.'

Hackett heeled on him. 'I said no, damn it! Tomorrow, you and your men will be riding to Adler Springs stage station to await the arrival of my daughter, and make sure she gets in all right. And for your information, I will be in command! Do I make myself clear?'

The news hit Kelso like a bucket of ice-water. He blinked twice as he digested what he'd been told, then, 'But, sir . . . '

'Get out!' Hackett snarled.

'I beg your pardon, major?'

'I said get out. I'll not have a subordinate stand in my office and question my orders. Especially if he's a damned drunk. Now get the hell out of my damned office!'

Without another word, Kelso turned and stormed out.

'Now, lieutenant,' said Hackett, 'where were we?'

★ ★ ★

'Seamus, do you have a minute?'

'Aye, cap'n,' Sergeant Seamus Murphy said, as he stopped polishing the buttons of his tunic. 'What can I do for you, sor?'

Murphy was a big Irishman from Dublin. He'd emigrated during his teenage years and joined the cavalry after the death of his parents. He had a shock of red hair and when it came down to fighting, a temper to match. But in Kelso's opinion, he was one of the best top-kicks on the post — apart from Shannon, of course.

'You're about to be ordered out on patrol with Lieutenant Reardon,' Kelso told him.

'Yes, sor,' was all Murphy said, but Kelso could see concern in the experienced man's eyes.

'Listen closely, Seamus,' Kelso said in a quiet tone, and proceeded to tell him about Lew's scouting mission. 'I tried to get the major to let me take my men, but he wants us to play nursemaid to his daughter.'

'And you're telling me all this . . . why, sor?'

'You need to pick the men for the patrol, Seamus. Pick the best fighting men 'A' Company has. Reardon's greener'n grass. He's got no experience, and the major seems set on putting me in my place.'

'I'll see to it, sor,' Murphy assured him. 'Keep an eye on the lieutenant, too.'

'And keep a tight rein on him. You don't want him riding to glory first time out.'

'I'll take care of it, sor.'

'Extra ammunition mightn't go astray either.'

'Yes, sor.'

'Stay safe, Seamus. Don't go being a hero out there.'

'You know me, sor. As soon as I see an Apache, I run away.'

Kelso left the sergeant to it and went to find Sergeant Mordecai Shannon.

★　★　★

'So Company 'C' lucks out again,' said Shannon, a thin, humorless smile on his face. 'Escort duty and a new commanding officer who, begging your pardon, couldn't find his backside with both hands. Looks to me like your idea to fight Apaches *like* Apaches was a

27

one-time thing, cap'n.'

There was no love lost between the two men. Moreover, Shannon frequently showed nothing but contempt for the man he considered a worthless drunk. Shannon was a bulky, moon-faced man with blue eyes, forty, with a lantern jaw and a prominent, pitted nose. If he didn't know Indians and the country as well as he did, Kelso would never have picked him for his command.

Ignoring the barb, Kelso said, 'Have the men ready to go early.'

'Fine,' Shannon acknowledged grudgingly.

'Have them take extra ammunition, just in case,' Kelso added. 'Have them strip their gear back to basics, same as before.'

'Why?' Shannon asked, bewildered. 'It's *over*, cap'n. The first time we went out there to fight the Apaches on their own terms was also the *last*. The major's not goin' to let you do it again.'

Kelso's eyes went flat. 'Just do it,

sergeant,' he hissed.

'Fine,' Shannon said again, and this time he spun on his heel and walked off.

★ ★ ★

The sun was low in the west when the detail of twenty-five men was ready to leave the post. The surrounding landscape was painted in shades of orange and purple as long fingers of light reached out across the cloud-streaked sky.

Kelso leaned against a porch upright in front of the officers' quarters and watched in silence as the command rode out the gate.

'They're headed for trouble, cap'n,' a deep voice said from beside him.

Without taking his eyes from the retreating line of riders, Kelso said, 'I know it. This is a job for us, Lew, not some green lieutenant.'

'Sarn't Murphy'll keep an eye on him,' Lew said.

'Sure he will. But this is the kind of job Company 'C' was *made* for.' He turned at last. 'You've heard we're riding out to Adler Springs to escort the stage in?'

'Uh-huh. Also heard that the major'll be in command.'

'You heard right.'

'Ever get the feelin' he don't trust you, cap'n?'

Kelso showed his teeth in a bitter smile. 'All the time, my friend. All the time.'

Standing downwind of Kelso enabled Lew to smell the fresh scent of rotgut on his breath.

'Might go aways if you gave up the bottle,' he observed mildly.

Kelso ignored that. 'Be ready to go early, Lew.'

'Yes, cap'n.'

Kelso went inside his quarters and slammed the door so hard it rattled the single window in the wall. He walked across to where he kept a battered trunk beside his bed, flipped the lid open and took out a full bottle of whiskey. He reached back in and grabbed a single, smeared glass. Then he closed the lid and walked across to the table in the center of the room. *Damn, I need this*, he thought, and filled the glass so that it almost overflowed.

He lifted it up to eye level and said, 'To Company 'C',' then he tossed it back in one go.

God, he thought. *How can something so good make me feel so damn bad?*

3

Somewhere in the town, a dog's bark split the crisp morning air. It was followed shortly thereafter by the crow of a rooster, heralding the new day. To the east, pink and red fingers of light showed as the sun clawed its way slowly into the cloudless desert sky.

The knock on Kelso's door was greeted with a deafening silence. The silence was shattered by the protesting shriek of dry hinges as the heavy door was reefed open.

Lew Eden's figure filled the doorway, his silhouette backlit by the dim light of dawn.

'Cap'n?' he called tentatively.

He was greeted by a series of irregular snores.

Stepping into the room, he found Kelso slumped over the table, a half-full glass sitting beside a bottle that had tipped onto its side and spilled the last miniscule amount onto the scarred surface.

'Cap'n?' Lew said, a little louder this time.

'Go 'way,' came the muffled reply.

'It's time to go, cap'n.'

'I said, go 'way.'

Looking around the room, Lew found what he was looking for and crossed to the washstand to retrieve it. He picked up the small, chipped pitcher and gave a satisfied nod as it sloshed. He returned to the table and emptied its contents over the captain's head.

Spluttering and wild-eyed, Kelso came to his feet with a bellow of rage. He fixed his angry stare on the scout and snarled, 'What the hell you think you're doing?'

The scout placed the empty pitcher gently on the scarred table, and in his deep baritone voice said, 'Company 'C' is ready.'

Kelso glared at him without speaking, water dripping from his nose. Lew waited for him to speak, but when the silence ensued, he shrugged, then turned and left.

★ ★ ★

'Good of you to join us, captain,' said Hackett, sarcasm dripping from every word. 'If you're quite ready, shall we go?'

'Yes, sir. Sorry, sir.'

Kelso had emerged from his quarters a few minutes after Lew had left. He wore a fresh uniform and had a canteen slung over his shoulder. He ran his gaze over the assembled men as they sat saddle waiting patiently for him to join them.

His eyes settled on Lane Carr. The man had once been a veterinarian but since the formation of Company 'C', he'd been learning all he could from Doc Sutton to double as a medic.

'Do you have all the medical supplies you need, Carr?' Kelso asked.

The thin thirty-year-old redhead

34

nodded. 'Yes, sir.'

Kelso's eyes wandered along the line of men who'd followed him into Sonora, what seemed like an age ago. Ruben Brady, the Texan, Veniamin (Benny) Baranski, the giant, bearded Cossack from the Ukraine. The small in stature Cyrus McGee, who'd been a jockey. Fitch, Quillan, and Napier, the list went on.

'If you're ready, Captain Kelso?' Hackett snapped impatiently.

Kelso climbed onto his horse and looked back to his commanding officer.

'Ready, sir.'

'Then get them moving, captain.'

'Yes, sir.' Kelso hipped around and called, '*Two's right, hoo-oo!*'

★ ★ ★

The old saying, 'You can lead a horse to water but you can't make him drink', was never truer than now, Seamus Murphy thought as the patrol rode single-file along the narrow strip of trail as it cut through a series of surrounding hills and low rock formations.

He'd warned Lieutenant Reardon about it, told him it would be better to go around, especially when he saw the faint dust cloud at the far end of the cutting as it drifted lazily skyward.

Reardon's reasoning for continuing was that if they were Beshe's broncos up ahead, then they would get away while they were 'dilly-dallying'. Murphy warned him it could be a trap, but Reardon would not be swayed.

Watchful eyes followed the steady progress of the blue line from in among the cactus and rocks. At the other end of the narrow trail, two braves rode around in circles with clumps of brush tied behind their horses. It had been a ruse used to draw the pony soldiers in, and it had worked perfectly.

Murphy's watchful eyes scanned the surrounding slopes looking for anything out the ordinary. He knew that the position was a perfect ambush site. He searched for a flicker of movement, a flash of color, something, anything.

And as he did so, Kelso's words echoed in his head. *Reardon's greener'n grass. Keep a tight rein on him. You don't want him riding to glory first time out.*

It was just then that a sharp hiss was followed by a dull thud as an Apache arrow sprouted from Reardon's chest.

The guttural moan he made was his only sound as he began to topple from his saddle. Behind Murphy another *thunk* indicated a second arrow strike — then the hills erupted with gunfire.

Almost before anyone knew it, the patrol was fighting for their lives amid a deadly crossfire.

'*Peters! Hanson! Check the lieutenant!*' Murphy barked, taking charge. '*The rest of you give covering fire!*'

More men fell to the withering hail of bullets and arrows. Murphy felt the burn of an arrow as it sliced through his shirt and opened a deep gash in his left shoulder. Through gritted teeth, he shouted, '*Prepare to move!*'

'What about the wounded?' another soldier yelled.

'Save those you can! And make it quick — I ain't dyin' here, not today!'

The two men detailed to check Reardon had him up and were carrying his limp body across to Murphy. 'He's still breathin', Sarge,' Peters told him.

'Quick, get him up here,' Murphy snapped.

They slung Reardon over the horse in front of Murphy, belly down.

'Get mounted and let's go,' said the sergeant. 'Bugler sound recall!'

The brassy tones rang out above the sounds of battle and the remaining cavalrymen answered its call. All ten of them. And some of those were wounded.

Finally, they broke free of the deadly trap and passed through the open end of the narrow trail. Looking back over his shoulder, Murphy saw what remained of his men and anger washed over him. He looked down at the unconscious lieutenant.

That's your one mistake, he thought.

If you live through this, you'd best learn from it.

A tall, rangy soldier rode up beside him and called out, 'Where we headed?'

'We'll keep on to the Anderson place,' Murphy shouted back. Hank Anderson had a small place around five miles from their position. It wasn't an overly productive spread but had a deep, sweet-water spring that never ran dry. Reardon had originally planned to stop and water the horses there then move on. Now it looked as though their stay would be a little longer than predicted. 'We can shelter there an' tend our wounded.'

The soldier looked back over his shoulder. 'You might want to ride a little faster then, Sarge.'

Murphy turned to check their back trail and spotted the dust cloud starting to rise. It looked as though Beshe and his broncos hadn't finished with them yet.

★ ★ ★

39

Some miles to the north, around mid-afternoon, Company 'C' was about to encounter a killer of a different type. This one first caused fever, then seizures, paralysis, hydrophobia, excessive salivation, and unusual aggression before finally inflicting an agonizing death.

Its name was *Rabies*.

The small column was moving at an easy lope along the stage trail when two coyotes burst out of some nearby brush. They made straight for the leading horses, snarling and yapping as they went. As they nipped at the horses' legs, Hackett's mount took fright and reared violently, dislodging him from the saddle. With a yelp of surprise, he fell and landed on the hard-packed earth in the middle of the road. His head struck an exposed rock, knocking him cold.

'Shoot the damned things!' Kelso ordered above the din.

Lew heeded the call and let off a shot, the impact of the bullet knocking one animal backwards with a pained yelp. The deafening report achieved a more satisfactory outcome than all the shouting and cursing had. The second creature turned and scampered back into the brush.

Its wounded companion attempted to regain its feet, still snarling and snapping. Flecks of foam flew from its mouth as it writhed in the dust. Another shot rang out and the rabid coyote fell still.

Dismounting, Kelso made a quick examination of Hackett and shouted, 'Carr, up front!'

The vet turned medic dismounted and came running. Without pause, he passed by Kelso and knelt beside the still form of his commanding officer.

Leaving him to his ministrations, Kelso turned to Mordecai Shannon. 'Have the men dismount, sergeant, and see they keep an eye for any other infected animal. If they see one, they shoot it dead, hear me? See that they're all okay and check to make sure the horses are all right, too.'

'Yo!'

'Lew?'

The scout moved his horse forward. 'Cap'n?'

'Go after that second coyote and kill it.'

Kelso turned his attention to Carr.

'How is he?' he asked.

'I'm not sure, sir,' Carr said, without looking up. 'He took a nasty fall and hit his head pretty hard. I'd like to get him back to the fort so's Doc Sutton could look him over, but it'll be dark before we get there. We really need to get him somewhere where he can be taken care of.'

'All right. Do what you can. I'll decide what to do with him when you're finished.'

'Yes, sir.'

'All the men and horses are fine,' Shannon said when he returned.

'That's something, at least.'

'How's the major doin'?'

'Carr's still looking him over. Tell the

42

men to stay sharp. If we've got hydrophobia out here, that's bad enough. I don't want the damned broncos attacking us while we're looking elsewhere.'

'Yo!'

Kelso crossed to where the dead coyote lay and gave it a closer inspection. It was emaciated, its fur matted, and its muzzle was dripping with foamy saliva. They were going to have to burn the carcass before they moved on, to make sure the coyote couldn't spread the infection to any predators who tried to eat it.

'Cap'n?' Carr spoke, breaking his train of thought.

'How's the major doing?'

'He's not good, sir,' Carr explained. 'That's the problem with a head injury like that. You can't really tell what's goin' on inside. We could move him and he could die, or we could stay put and he could die anyway. I wish Doc Sutton was here, sir.'

'Well, he's not, and you're all Major

Hackett has. Doc Sutton trained you for working in the field. I have confidence that you'll do the right thing. Now, there is a place southeast of here. If I dispatch you and some of the men there, do you think he'll make it?'

'I don't know, sir.'

Kelso nodded grimly. 'OK. Get him ready to travel.' He looked for Shannon and saw him speaking with Baranski and Fitch. When he was finished, the two soldiers mounted their horses and rode off to higher ground to gain a clearer picture of the surrounding desert.

'Sergeant Shannon,' Kelso called.

The big man hurried over and stopped in front of him. 'Yes, sir?'

'I want you, Carr, and four other men to take Major Hackett to the Anderson place southeast of here.'

'Is that wise, sir?'

'Well, we're damned if we do and damned if we don't. Carr says that any movement could kill the major, and if we wait here and do nothing, then he could die anyway.'

'Be mighty convenient if he didn't, wouldn't it?' Shannon said softly.

Kelso's gaze turned flinty. 'I'll forget you said that, Sergeant. Now, do as I ordered.'

There was a drawn-out pause before Shannon said through gritted teeth, 'Yes, sir.'

4

Lew returned fifteen minutes later and reported back to Kelso.

'Coyote's dead,' he said. 'And I left the body to burn. But hydrophobia . . . '

Kelso nodded. 'I know. It changes everything. I'm sending Shannon, Carr and some others to the Anderson place so Carr can take care of the major. We'll continue on to Adler Springs to meet the stage and escort it in.'

Lew nodded but remained silent.

'Something on your mind, Lew?'

'No, cap'n.'

Kelso turned. 'Sergeant!'

Taking his time, Shannon approached the two men.

'Yeah?' he said.

Overlooking the blatant disrespect, Kelso asked, 'Have you picked your men?'

'I'm takin' Baranski, Napier, Morse, and Edwards.'

'Fine. Watch yourselves on the way to Anderson's. We don't know yet how far this rabies epidemic has spread.'

'Might be better if we all stick together, then,' said Shannon.

'Uh-uh. The rest of us will go on to meet the stage.'

An incredulous look came over the sergeant's face. 'You're goin' to split your force at a time like this?'

'It can't be helped.'

'The hell it can't! We got two different bands of renegades causin' all kinds of havoc out there, plus this damn hydrophobia, and you want to split your force?'

'That's enough, sergeant!' Kelso hissed. 'Those are my orders.'

Shannon glared at him. 'Damn you, you've been at the booze again, ain't you? Where is it? In that canteen of yours?'

Kelso's eyes flickered a touch.

'So, that's it,' said Shannon. Wheeling

around, he stamped over to Kelso's horse.

'Sergeant!' Kelso snapped.

Shannon ignored him and kept going. Kelso opened his mouth and took a step forward but Lew put a hand on his arm. Under the watchful eyes of all present, the sergeant unhitched the canteen and fumbled with its lid.

He put it to his nose and his expression changed. He smelled it again in case he'd missed it the first time.

'Satisfied, Sergeant?' Kelso inquired.

Shannon's face turned red. 'I know you got it stashed somewhere.'

Squaring his shoulders, Kelso grated, 'Attend to your duties, sergeant.'

After the canteen was hung back up and Shannon stormed off, Kelso turned to Lew and asked, 'When did you switch it?'

'An hour back, when we stopped to water the horses.'

'Thanks.'

'I don't want your thanks,' Lew whispered harshly. 'If your drinkin' gets you kicked out of this man's army, you've only got yourself to blame. The truth, cap'n? You probably deserve it. But when it starts to affect your thinkin', when you make a bad decision that's like to get us all killed, that's when I take it personal. Right about now, I'm the only friend you got. You're a good commander, but you could be more. If you want this Company 'C' business of yours to work, get rid of the damned bottle before you get everyone killed. Now, do you still want to split your command?'

Flushing, knowing every word Lew had said was the stone-cold truth, Kelso nodded. 'Yes. There's no other way. Hackett needs tending, and we still need to get to Adler Springs.'

Eden nodded. 'All right. Split your force. Me, I'll go see if I can get a line on Beshe . . . or Bodaway. They're the last sonsabitches we need to run into right now. If I can find 'em, I'll report back and you can avoid 'em.'

'When you're done, swing by the

Anderson place,' Kelso told him. 'I'll detour the stage there to pick the major up. If we're not there, make your way back to Whitethorn.'

With the decision made, the two groups, and Lew, went their separate ways. None of them knew they would be tested as never before over the coming days.

★   ★   ★

As they rode out, Private Wilson said, 'Hey, McGee — what's this thing, rabies?'

'You mean you don't know?'

'I know it's what sent those coyotes crazy, but that's about all.'

McGee said, 'Well, if it comes to it, I don't guess I know a whole lot myself. I know that was any one of us to get bit by the rabid animal, we'd be pretty sure to get it ourselves.'

'An' then?' prodded Wilson.

'Then he's take sick and die.'

'I was up north when the Sioux were

kickin' up a fuss,' said Fitch. 'Ran into an old scout up there who told me how once a pack of wolves fed on an infected carcass. It took a while, but once it started there was hell to pay.'

'What happened?' Wilson asked eagerly.

'From what I was told, that pack started huntin' a bunch of folks that was in the area at the time. Out of six, only one managed to reach a town. He staggered in late one day, clothes hanging from his body. It was too late for him, though. He'd been bitten pretty bad, and it wasn't long before he started actin' like the wolves that killed his friends.'

'Really?' Wilson blurted out.

'Really,' said Fitch. 'So don't go takin' no chances. First chance you get, you kill a rabid animal stone-dead, 'fore he can kill you.'

* * *

Adler Springs stage station sat in a natural bowl-shaped depression surrounded by a dry and hostile wilderness consisting predominantly of giant saguaros, cholla, and burr sage. Large rocks broke up the green and insinuated their own particular hue to the mix. At the bottom of the two-hundred-foot concavity was the spring from which the station drew its water and its name.

The stage trail topped the east ridge and traveled downslope, cutting back on itself a couple of times before straightening out at the bottom. From there it ran a rugged mile through the rough terrain and up the other side, repeating a path not dissimilar to the one it had taken on the way down.

The Adler Springs station itself was a small jumble of adobe buildings which consisted of the station house, a small trading post/saloon, stables, and a corral. It was also utilized as a stopover by the dubious and questionable characters who passed through on their way south.

When the afternoon stage topped the rise, rail-thin Ben Pardoe knew instantly that something was wrong. The pace it was travelling on approach to the dangerous switchbacks was way too fast to negotiate safely . . . and then he heard the gunfire. The driver up top sawed on the reins, willing the six-horse team around the first turn. He stood hard on the brake, locking the wheel as he tried desperately to prevent the stage from careening over the edge.

Beside him, the guard twisted to face the rear, his legs wrapped around the seat tightly and fired his rifle at an unseen enemy. A moment later, only a short distance behind the speeding coach, a large force of Apaches thundered over the rim, their war cries sending a cold shiver down Pardoe's spine.

Turning his attention from the impending onslaught, he rushed from where he had been readying the fresh team to raise help from the station house. 'Molly! Molly!'

His wife of twenty years, a tall

woman with dark hair, emerged from inside.

'What is it?' she called.

'Apaches!' he shouted. 'Get the rifles.'

It was only then that the gunshots registered for Molly Pardoe. She looked out along the trail and saw the stage tilt wildly as it negotiated the second turn. Her hand flew to her mouth as she whispered, 'Oh, my Lord.'

Ben's voice broke through her frozen state of shock.

'Molly! The rifles!'

She whirled about, the hems of her gray dress flicking up. Once inside, she went to the gun rack on the far wall where she took down two Winchester rifles and grabbed two boxes of ammunition.

It wasn't the first time that they'd had to fight off Indians, but the feeling of dread, deep down in the pit of Molly's stomach, told her that this time was going to be different.

Ben met her at the door and she

passed him a rifle and ammunition. He kissed her roughly on the cheek and said, 'Lock yourself in.'

'But . . . ' she started.

'Just do it!' he snapped and turned away from the door as Molly shut and barred it behind him.

Ben turned to look at the stage as it approached the final bend before the trail flattened out for the run in. The Apaches were almost on top of it. He figured there to be somewhere near thirty warriors, maybe more. He watched in horror as the guard threw up his arms and fell forward from the top of the stage. The man's body struck the deeply rutted trail in front of the left front wheel which ran right over him as the coach continued its bouncing forward momentum.

The driver stood on the brake once more to take the final turn but found that it no longer worked. As the team turned the tight bend, the stage tipped precariously. The driver sensed that this was it and leaped from the driving seat just as the conveyance reached the point of no return and went over.

The team of horses broke free from their bonds to the Concord when it hit the hard ground, digging in and sending up a large cloud of dust.

Ben saw the driver stagger to his feet. He was immediately swarmed by the following Apaches. The station manager opened fire with the Winchester, and he heard Molly do the same from inside.

Good girl, he said to himself as he saw one of the Indians fall from his horse. He fired two more shots and a half-naked warrior died as a slug plowed into his chest. A shout from a warrior drew his attention and he saw a gathering of five or six warriors huddled together. One of them pointed in Ben's direction and they kicked their mounts savagely and rode towards him.

He jacked another round into the Winchester's breech and lined the foresight up on the leading rider's chest. Ben squeezed the trigger and the rifle whiplashed, its recoil driving back against his shoulder.

Through the small cloud of blue-gray gun smoke that exploded from the Winchester's barrel, Ben saw the Apache disappear over his horse's rump.

An angry cry escaped the lips of another Indian. This one was armed with a battered Spencer which he raised and fired. Ben felt the impact of the .56 caliber slug and his right leg kicked out from beneath him, spilling his slight frame to the hard-packed earth.

A loud, anguished shout escaped his lips. He managed to drag himself back to his feet and bring the Winchester up. He levered the action again and fired a shot from his hip. It missed and he levered in another round.

In the background, he heard Molly's rifle firing and told himself, *She's a fighter that one.*

Suddenly, another ten or so warriors broke away from the main bunch, angling towards the stage station.

A burning pain lanced through Ben

Pardoe's chest. He looked down at the Apache arrow that protruded from his torso. Another drove deep into his chest and Ben Pardoe could feel the strength leave his body. He collapsed to his knees as everything around him grew dark. He slumped forward and with a dry snap, both arrow shafts broke off.

The last thing Ben Pardoe heard were the distant screams of a woman.

'Molly . . . ' he gasped, then died.

But the screams he'd heard hadn't come from his wife. These had been emitted by a young lady in a blue dress who was being dragged from the wrecked stage. Ben wasn't to know, but Molly was already dead.

★   ★   ★

Gunfire sounded across the late afternoon, and Shannon quickly ordered his small detail off the trail and had them hide the horses behind a clump of brush.

There was no change in Hackett's

condition, which was good but also bad. Good because he was still alive, bad because there'd been no improvement. He'd been riding double with Benny Baranski, the big Ukrainian holding him in place as they headed for shelter. They now placed him gently in the sparse shade of a bush so the men could investigate.

Shannon, Baranski, and Carr bellied up a slight incline and peered over the rise. Before them was the Anderson place, and it was under siege.

'I guess we can rule this place out,' Carr observed. 'There ain't no way we're gettin' in there.'

The homestead was surrounded. Firing positions were marked by puffs of gun smoke, and from where they lay, they could see that they were out-gunned and almost overrun.

'Look,' Baranski said urgently. 'Near the corral.'

Shannon looked and saw a man in a blue uniform.

'Do you see?' Baranski asked.

'Yeah, I see,' Shannon acknowledged.

'And there beside the wagon,' Baranski pointed out. 'That is . . . '

'Seamus Murphy,' Shannon finished for him.

'That's the patrol down there,' Carr said.

'What's left of it,' Shannon stated. 'There ain't enough gunfire comin' outta there to be a full compliment.'

'They must've run into trouble somewhere and taken shelter here,' Carr observed.

'What are we going to do?' Baranski asked.

'We're goin' to break through the Apache perimeter and help them out,' Shannon told them. 'The broncos have them penned up nicely. But a few more guns could make all the difference.' He looked pointedly at Carr. 'You know what it means for the major. Can he stand it?'

Carr shrugged. 'I can't say. He's stood it this far. I guess that's somethin'.'

'You'll be right to carry him a little further, Benny?'

Baranski shook his head. 'You carry him. I lead. Show them how Cossack fights.'

He thumped his chest to emphasize the point.

'All right, let's do it.'

A few minutes later they were back in the saddle and ready to go.

'Lead out Benny,' Shannon said. He turned to the others. 'Don't stop for anythin'. You do, they'll kill you.'

5

When Seamus Murphy saw Benny Baranski top the rise, he felt a surge of relief flood through his weary body. What remained of the patrol had been fighting Beshe's bronco Apaches for most of the afternoon.

Murphy had seven men left. Of those, two were wounded, and he himself was carrying a flesh wound from their earlier encounter. Lieutenant Reardon was barely alive. The occupants of the Anderson spread, John Anderson, his wife Betty, their two grown sons, Luther and Simon, and their daughter, Muriel, had fought valiantly so far, but Luther and his father were now wounded and incapable of fighting.

Next over the rise came Napier, followed by Morse and the others.

And that was it.

Murphy waited for the rest of Company 'C' to gallop to their rescue, but they never appeared. His relief turned to bitter disappointment when he realized that his envisaged reinforcements were limited to this small handful of men.

'Damn it,' he cursed and recommenced firing at the near invisible enemy.

⋆　⋆　⋆

When Benny Baranski hit the outer perimeter of the Apache cordon, two of them seemingly leaped from the desert and launched themselves at the big Cossack. With a roar of what could be considered enjoyment, Baranski rode the first one down with his horse while he swung a ham-sized fistful of Colt that connected with the side of his other attacker's head. He heard a dull crack and the Apache dropped to the ground.

'*Narakhovuvaty!*' he bellowed. 'Charge!'

More Apaches appeared, sprouting like wildflowers from behind brush and rocks. They concentrated their fire on the newcomers and Baranski could hear the loud snaps as bullets passed close by. Another half-naked warrior appeared in front of his racing mount and the Ukrainian fired a shot from his six-gun. The Apache cried out and spun around. He fell in a heap off to the side as the small procession of riders thundered past.

It was then that Company 'C' lost its first man. An arrow bit deep into Morse's chest and dislodged him from his fast-running mount. There was no shout from him, no cry of pain. He just slid sideways from his saddle and hit the ground dead.

Finally, the rest of the riders entered the yard and Shannon drew up in front of the adobe house. With Carr's help, they got Hackett inside the building where the Company 'C' medic could work on him.

Next, Shannon went back outside

and found Murphy still sheltering behind the wagon. There was dried blood on his uniform, and he had a fresh graze to his side from a close call with a bullet, and a thin trickle of blood oozed from a small cut on his cheek caused by a wooden splinter.

'Just when you need the cavalry, you lot is all we get,' the Irishman said, his voice dripping with sarcasm.

'You fellers look like you've had a hard time of it, Seamus,' Shannon observed.

Murphy fired at a fleeting figure out in the desert. 'We left good men on our back-trail, Mordecai,' he said. 'Where's Kelso?'

'He's headed for Adler Springs to meet the stage.'

Murphy absorbed that, then asked: 'Was that the major you brought in?'

'Yeah.'

Between shots, Shannon filled him in on what had happened.

'I'd say he didn't reach that decision lightly,' Murphy allowed when Shannon cursed at the splitting of the force.

'It was damned stupid.'

'Kelso might be a lot of things, Mordecai, but stupid ain't one of them. I would have rather he'd been leadin' our patrol this mornin' than the lieutenant.'

Another flurry of shots to their front brought a string of curses from Baranski. It also brought a thin smile to Murphy's lips.

'How long have you been here, Seamus?' Shannon asked.

'Too damned long,' came the reply. 'We're runnin' low on ammunition and water.'

Shannon frowned. 'How is it you're low on water?'

'Beshe had one of his warriors slit a hog's throat and dump it in the spring to poison the water,' Murphy explained. 'All we got is what's in our canteens and some inside.'

'How many men have you got left?'

'Five able to fight plus Simon Anderson, his mother, and sister. I got two wounded inside. One of them is Reardon.'

'Is he goin' to make it?'

Murphy shrugged. 'Who knows?'

'How many Apaches you figure Beshe has?' Shannon asked.

'Somewhere between fifteen and twenty,' Murphy guessed. 'We accounted for a couple so I'd say closer to fifteen than twenty. Although Baranski took care of some on the way in. That damned Cossack is crazy, I swear.'

The firing ceased abruptly, allowing a heavy silence to descend over the darkening battleground.

'What do you think is goin' on?' Shannon asked.

'Maybe they're tired,' Murphy said cynically.

'Sarge, we got a problem.'

Both Shannon and Murphy turned to look at Carr.

'And if I can't fix it then the major will die.'

★ ★ ★

Shannon paled and his voice sounded loud in the confines of the small homestead. 'You're kidding,' he said softly.

'If I don't do it, he'll die,' Carr told him again.

'But you could *kill* him by doin' it!' Murphy pointed out.

'It's a good bet that's what will happen, yes,' said Carr with a nod.

'And you're goin' to have to . . . ?' Shannon's voice trailed away.

'Open up his head, yes,' Carr confirmed.

'Can you do it?' Murphy asked.

'I guess we'll find out. I have instruments in my saddlebags that'll do the job. And Doc Sutton did one a month ago on a drunk cowboy who'd been kicked in the head by a horse. I was there when he did it.'

'Didn't he die?' Shannon asked pointedly.

'Yes, he did,' Carr allowed. 'But I watched what he did and I think I can do it.'

'You *think*?' Murphy asked.

'Listen, either way, he could die. If I don't at least try it, he'll die for sure.'

Shannon looked at Murphy. 'What do you think?'

The Irishman shrugged. 'I guess some chance is better than no chance at all.'

'What did you say it was called again?' Shannon asked.

'Trephination.'

'And you have to drill a hole in his head to relieve the pressure?'

'Yes.'

Shannon let his breath go in a rush. 'All right, do it. I'll stick to fightin' Apaches. Seems to me that might be safer than what you're about to do.'

Carr swallowed nervously and said, 'I'll get right to it.'

'Before you go,' Murphy said, stopping him. 'How's Lieutenant Reardon?'

'He's holding on . . . just about. If he's still alive when the sun comes up tomorrow, then he'll make it.'

Murphy nodded. 'Thanks.'

'I'll go and get ready.'

They watched him go and Shannon said grudgingly, 'He's the one good thing that Kelso has done for this outfit.'

'How so?'

'Ever since the company was formed, Kelso had him learnin' from Doc Sutton. Just in case one of us got hurt and we needed tendin'. He's kinda like a field surgeon.'

'Sounds like a good idea.'

'C'mon,' said Shannon. 'Let's do a check outside.'

* * *

'Did you hear it?' Napier asked Baranski.

'Mmm,' the big Cossack grunted, staring intently out into the surrounding darkness.

The sun hadn't been down long and the moon wasn't up yet, so the land was pretty much as black as pitch.

'What do you think it was?' Napier whispered.

Baranski shook his head and said, 'Get Shannon.' He then crept forward and disappeared into the inky blackness.

Napier hurried off to find his sergeant.

He found him with Murphy by the corral, where Edwards was stationed.

'Sarge! Sarge!' he hissed.

Shannon wheeled on him. 'What is it?'

'Benny's gone out.'

'What?'

'We heard somethin' in the darkness in front of our position, and before I could stop him he went out to take a look.'

'Damn fool Cossack,' Shannon swore, and together he and Murphy followed Napier back to where the pair had been positioned.

They got about halfway when a sudden, pained scream pierced the night and the three men brought up their weapons.

'Do you think that was Benny?' asked Napier.

'Get around the rest of the men and have them stand to,' Shannon ordered. 'And make it quick.'

No sooner had he run off when movement in front of Shannon and Murphy caused them to raise their guns ready to fire. Baranski emerged from the darkness, dragging the body of a dead bronco.

'Scout,' the big Cossack grunted.

'Don't do that again,' Shannon snapped. 'There ain't enough of us for you to go galavantin' about in the dark. Now, get back to your post and stay there.'

'Yep,' said Murphy after the Cossack and his macabre trophy had gone. 'I wouldn't mind one of him in my troop.'

'He keeps doin' that, he won't be alive to be in *any* troop. It looks like it's goin' to be a long night.'

★ ★ ★

Kelso drew the small detail to a halt when a rider appeared out of the darkness in front of them. He knew it had to be bad news. For the past two hours, he'd been expecting to meet the stage along the way to Adler Springs. When it hadn't materialized, he'd sent Brady on ahead to scout.

Now, with Brady's return, a feeling of dread settled on his shoulders.

'It's bad, cap'n.'

A chill ran down Kelso's spine as the cold night air pricked his skin. 'How bad?'

'They're all dead. Those that I could find anyway,' Brady reported. 'But it was dark and hard to tell.'

'Indians?'

'Yes, sir,' Brady said.

'Was there any sign of the major's daughter?'

'No, sir. Not that I looked around much. It was dark.'

Kelso nodded. 'All right, Brady. We'll camp here tonight and have a look tomorrow. I don't want to go riding

73

into an ambush in the middle of the night.'

'Who do you figure it was, sir?' asked the trooper.

'I've no idea. But it'll either be Beshe's broncos or the Mimbreños. Like you say — we won't know until it gets light. Anyway, let's get a camp set up and we'll worry about it later.'

'Yes, sir.'

Kelso hipped in the saddle and ran his gaze over the dark shadows behind him. 'We'll camp here for the night.'

'What about the stage, cap'n?' Quillan asked.

'It doesn't matter anymore,' Kelso told him. 'We're too late.'

6

They came out of the darkness like wraiths, closing on the Anderson place from all directions. Without a sound, the broncos slashed the throats of one of Murphy's remaining soldiers and Simon Anderson. The latter emitted a strangled cry that barely reached Seamus Murphy's ears. However, it was enough to warn him that something wasn't right.

At the time, he was propped against the wagon wheel, dozing. The unnatural sound brought him awake and when he came to his feet, he was attacked by a bronco Apache who launched himself out of the darkness.

The hard, wiry body crashed into Murphy and knocked him off his feet. The pair grappled as they rolled about on the hard ground in a fight to the death. The Apache snarled wildly as he fought to kill the hated white-eye. The razor-sharp knife he held scored a line across the Irishman's forearm and caused Murphy to gasp at the burning pain.

Murphy grabbed the Apache's sinewy knife arm in a vice-like grip, thus preventing the needle-sharp point from plunging deep into his throat. The bronco brought his weight to bear trying to force the weapon down.

But the big Irishman was as strong as a bull and held the Indian's weight. Keeping hold of the Apache's knife arm in his left hand, he reached with his right hand to free his sidearm. The triple-click of the hammer going back was the first indication to the bronco that he was in trouble.

In desperation, he tried to roll away from the hard barrel as it drove into his side. The sound of the gunshot filled the darkness. The apache grunted as the bullet smashed into him from close range. He stiffened and went still.

Seamus rolled him off and scrambled

to his feet. From the darkness to his front another warrior appeared. Murphy snapped off a couple of shots, killing the knife-wielding intruder. He then opened his mouth and roared at the top of his voice, '*Stand to! Apaches inside the perimeter!*'

* * *

Mordecai Shannon was inside the homestead when the first shots were fired and the warning shout from Murphy sounded. He had been watching Carr carry out his work on Hackett with morbid fascination. Assisting Carr was Betty Anderson and her daughter Muriel.

Carr had been at it for well over an hour, using one of his surgical irons — to Shannon it looked more like a chisel with a flat end — to slowly shape a dollar-sized hole in the major's skull, just above his hairline. The purpose of the procedure was to relieve the build-up of pressure on the brain following Hackett's injury — at least, that was how Carr tried to explain it. He was also confident that, if Hackett lived, the bone would slowly grow back to cover the hole.

'You're kiddin',' Shannon had breathed.

'No, sarge . . . ' Carr continued as he worked on his patient. 'If this works, the bone'll grow back.'

Now, hearing the sounds of battle coming from outside, Shannon snapped, 'Damn it!' and ran towards the door.

Outside, the firing escalated and the war cries of the attacking Indians filtered in. Carr looked at Muriel Anderson and said, 'Get my sidearm from my holster over there on the chair.'

She gave him an alarmed look but did as she was asked. Once she had it in her hand he said, 'Now, anyone who comes through that door that ain't a soldier, you shoot.'

'Except your brother,' her mother warned her.

'I . . . I can't,' she stammered.

'Put it this way, girlie. If you don't, then we're all as good as dead.'

As if on cue, the door smashed back and a paint-daubed Apache burst into the room. Muriel Anderson raised the six-gun and closed her eyes.

★   ★   ★

The battle raged for ten minutes, much of it dominated by gunshots and violent hand-to-hand fighting. When it was over, an eerie silence descended across the yard. In the middle of it stood Shannon and Murphy. The Irishman, in addition to his previous flesh wounds, had a thin line of blood trickling down his left cheek from a small cut just below the hairline.

Shannon, on the other hand, had a large bloodstain on his pants leg and a painful limp to accompany it. Embedded deeply in the muscle was an arrowhead with a short portion of the shaft protruding.

79

'How many did we lose?' Shannon asked through gritted teeth.

'The young Anderson feller is gone, and I lost one from my troop with another wounded,' the Irishman told him. 'And Edwards from your lot.'

That made it two men Company 'C' had lost in a matter of hours, Shannon reflected bitterly.

'What about the broncos?' he asked.

'There can't be many of them left,' Murphy theorized. 'Not after that. I counted ten dead Apaches inside the perimeter alone.'

'Let's hope you're right,' Shannon grimaced. 'I don't think we could take another attack like that one.'

'Might pay you to get off that leg,' Murphy pointed out.

'Yeah.' Shannon winced again. 'You're probably right.'

Shannon limped across to the station and went inside. He almost fell over the Apache's corpse just inside the doorway. He looked down at it, then up at Carr, who was still busy working on

Hackett. The medic sensed Shannon's eyes on him and said, 'It was the girl. She did a mighty fine job stoppin' him.'

'Yeah, looks like,' Shannon grunted and looked over at Muriel.

She sat on a chair, visibly shaken and traumatized by the knowledge that she had taken another human life.

'Could you have a look at this leg of mine, miss?' he asked, figuring to distract her from her thoughts. 'It kinda hurts like a bi — like gangbusters. If you could I'd appreciate it.'

She continued to sit, as though she had not heard him.

'Miss? Excuse me miss . . . '

Her head came up and she looked to see who had spoken to her. 'I'm sorry, did you say something?'

He repeated his request to her and she gave him a wan smile then rose to her feet.

She took one look at the wound and when she saw the protrusion of the broken shaft, she gasped. 'Come and sit down,' Muriel Anderson said to him.

Once seated, he looked at Carr. 'I take it that you ain't killed him yet?' he said.

'Give me time, Sarge, give me time.'

'When you're done there with your experimentin', you may need to cut this arrow outta my leg.'

'Join the line,' Carr said without pause and continued to work.

★ ★ ★

Something moved in the brush to his left and Private Wilson jumped. Damn Fitch and his stories.

It was sometime after midnight and the moon sat like a giant silver orb in a cloudless sky. He was in his second hour of watch, and had jumped at just about every sound.

The sound came again. This time it was off to his left. Wilson dropped his hand to the flap of his cavalry issue holster.

'Come on you bastard,' he murmured, 'let's get a look at you.'

The next sound came from his left again and a flutter of alarm raced through him. Wilson brought his Colt free and cocked it, the loud triple-click of the hammer sounding unnaturally loud in the clear night air. Whatever it was, it was stalking him.

His mouth was instantly dry and he noticed a thin trickle of sweat running down his forehead, even though the night was chilled.

Then . . . nothing.

Everything was silent again. Wilson heard only his own heavy breathing. He relaxed, eased down the gun hammer and put the six-gun back in its holster.

At that moment, the brush exploded and a snarling, enraged, black shadow shot forward at blinding speed and launched at Wilson. The soldier let out an involuntary scream as he clawed at the butt of his sidearm.

Compared to the creature attacking him, Wilson was painfully slow, and the rabid javelina latched on to the lower part of his right leg and began to savage it. Wilson's screams grew frantic as he tried to make the desert pig let go. He cursed it, shouted at it, belted it with a fist and the barrel of his sidearm, too afraid to think of shooting it.

And still, the javelina kept on.

A gunshot followed by a sharp yelp rocked the night. The javelina was knocked onto its side and lay unmoving, dribbling froth from its slack mouth. Out of the darkness came Kelso and the rest of the men, weapons at the ready.

'*I'm gonna die! I'm gonna die!*' Wilson ranted. '*It bit me. I'm gonna die!*'

'Easy there, Wilson,' said Kelso. 'Let's get you into the firelight and have a look.'

'It bit me, damn it!' shrieked Wilson.

'Maybe not,' Kelso said hopefully.

'I ain't goin' to end up like them coyotes,' Wilson said in a calmer tone.

Kelso pointed to a couple of men. 'Carry him over to the fire.'

Before anyone could do anything,

Wilson looked at McGee and with a sorrowful shake of his head, raised the six-gun in his hand, placed it against his temple, and pulled the trigger.

It wasn't until the sun came up the following morning that it became evident that Wilson's cavalry boot had been the only thing damaged in the coyote's attack.

7

The following morning was cold even when the sun came up. The air held a crispness that made Kelso pull his jacket collar up to retain his body heat. They'd buried Wilson and moved from their bivouac before dawn, and reached Adler Springs soon after sunrise.

The detail sat on the rim of the bowl and waited while Kelso scanned the surrounding area with his field glasses. His gaze wandered from the far rim to the upturned stage, and finally to the station itself.

In the yard, he could see the body of Ben Pardoe, sprawled where it had fallen. He located two more bodies which must be those of the passengers. One had been stripped naked and tied to a stage wheel. The other, also naked, had been fastened to a saguaro cactus. Further investigation revealed the bodies of the driver and the guard.

Kelso lowered the glasses and licked his lips. What he would give for a drink right now. Instead, he said, 'Brady, take Teeters and Ankrum with you and look around the stage. I'll take the others with me. Once you've checked it out, get the bodies together and we'll bury them before we move out.'

'Yes, sir.'

Before they headed down to the Adler Springs station, Kelso left Mike Quillan up on the rim to act as a lookout. With that done, they rode forward at an even pace until they reached the bottom.

Once there, Kelso had them fan out to check for any survivors. Of course, there were none. Pardoe and his wife Molly were both dead. Pardoe had been mutilated after death while Molly hadn't been touched. She lay beside her fallen rifle, death evident from the blackened hole where her right eye used to be. The Apaches must have carried off their dead and wounded, if there had been any.

Kelso called across to Porter Fitch, 'Find a shovel and start burying these bodies.'

Still subdued following the suicide of his buddy, Wilson, Fitch said only, 'Sir.'

They commenced their somber task and soon after, Brady rode over to make his report. He handed his commanding officer an arrow taken from one of the bodies. It was Mimbreño. 'They're all dead over there, sir. And there's no sign of the girl.'

Kelso nodded. 'So, we can assume that they've taken her.'

'Yes, sir.'

'How are your scouting skills?'

'Fair, sir.'

'All right. While we finish up here, I want you to pick up their trail until you get a general direction of where they're headed. After that, come back here and we'll head for the Anderson spread to link up with Sergeant Shannon.'

'We're not goin' to follow them, sir?' Brady inquired.

'Not in the state we're in. If we go after them, I want the rest of the company first.'

Brady bit off whatever he was about to say and frowned. Then, 'Sir, look.'

Kelso turned and looked to where Brady was pointing. Up on the rim, Quillan was signaling. He looked back at Brady and said, 'Carry on, but don't go too far. There could be trouble.'

'Yes, sir.'

Kelso climbed onto his horse and rode up to the rim, where Quillan awaited him.

'What is it?' he asked.

'Look, out there,' said Quillan, pointing to the northeast.

Following his track, Kelso saw what had him worried. Curling lazily into the sky about a mile distant was a thin column of pale smoke.

'Over there, too,' Quillan said, pointing to the north.

Kelso looked and found another one.

'Keep an eye out, and if you see anything that I should know about, come find me.'

'Yes, sir.'

* * *

As soon as Brady topped the ridge, he saw the smoke too. It made him hesitate, unsure whether to continue or not. After a moment of indecision, he set his mouth in a thin line and eased his horse forward.

He let it continue for about a mile before he stopped beside a large rock formation. Here, he took his Springfield and dismounted. Then he climbed as high as he could to survey the surrounding landscape.

The two lazy columns still drifted skyward, but something else caught his attention. To the northeast, he saw a faint smudge of dust looming just above the ground. Nothing big, maybe two riders. He watched it for a time before climbing back down.

Brady started back for the station without haste and when he reached the rim he spotted something out of place. Once more he dismounted and walked over to a small prickly pear and bent down. He retrieved the item and studied it.

Fabric.

Blue material from a woman's dress.

It would indicate that Major Hackett's daughter was still alive. But for how long?

★   ★   ★

It took almost two hours to bury the dead, by which time Brady had returned.

'They headed northeast, sir,' he explained. 'My guess is that they're headed towards the Santa Rita mountains.' He also told Kelso about the dust he'd seen. 'My guess would be scouts left behind to watch their back trail. I'd say they know we're here.'

Nodding, Kelso said, 'Get ready to move out.'

'There's one other thing, sir,' Brady added.

'Which is . . . ?'

He reached into his pocket and pulled out a piece of pale-blue material. Kelso examined it and concluded that it had come from a woman's dress.

'Where did you find it?'

'At the top of the rim. It could be a sign she's still alive, sir.'

'All right. Get ready to pull out.'

'Are we goin' after them?'

'No, we're headed back to the Anderson spread.'

Brady hesitated before saying, 'I would've thought we'd be goin' after them Indians to get her back.'

Kelso fixed him with a hard look. He knew that Brady was thinking just like all the others — that Kelso's boozing had clouded his judgment. But there was no point in biting Brady's head off about it. Kelso couldn't blame the men for the way they thought. God knew, he'd given them all enough cause.

Instead he said, 'We'll be doing that in due course. But first we're heading for Anderson's.'

He looked down at the material in his hand. The hand was shaking. God, he needed a drink.

But that could wait. His priority now was the major's daughter. He had to get the girl back . . . and the only way he could do that was to put Company 'C' back together again.

* * *

After a while it had become clear to Lew Eden that the tracks he'd picked up were leading him straight to the Anderson place. He knew the Andersons vaguely, and it made his blood run cold to think what he might find when he got there.

Now, keeping out of sight as best he could, he studied the place. He had counted eight live Apaches in cover around the ranch house, but it was hard to know who'd had the worst of the fighting, for the yard was littered with as many dead soldiers as dead Indians.

As he thought about the Andersons, wondering if they were holed up safe, he was unaware of movement off to his right. In his initial inspection of the ranch, he had failed to see a lone Apache who was operating as a lookout in case another group of bluecoats should come out of the desert. Now, the half-naked, paint-daubed warrior was slowly working his way towards Lew with a knife in his right fist.

The Indian's moccasins barely made a sound on the desert sand as he stalked his quarry. His skin glistened with sweat as the sun beat down. He had closed the gap to within ten feet when Lew turned around.

He didn't know what had made him turn. It might have been the soft squeak of moccasin on sand, or the way the hairs on the back of his neck stood up as a tingle ran down his spine. Whatever it was, it warned him that all was not right, and he turned just in time to prevent his death.

The Apache leaped at the prone scout, but Lew managed to get an arm up to block the downward sweep of the wicked looking blade before it could find a place in his throat.

The Apache grunted in surprise at his failed attempt to kill. He raised his knife arm again, but a strong black hand took his wrist in a painful grip. His eyes widened as Lew twisted the arm savagely, causing him to drop the knife. The scout then brought up his fist and smashed it into the side of the Indian's head.

The first blow seemed to have little impact, so Lew hit him again. The second stunned the Apache and Lew hurled him aside.

Cat-like, both men sprang to their feet. Somehow the bronco had managed to regain possession of his knife and now stood crouched ready to attack once more. Without taking his eyes off his opponent, Lew reached down and took his stone-headed hatchet from its beaded sheath.

'*Pronto se unirá sus hermanos, comedor de perro,*' Lew growled. 'You will soon join your brothers, Dog Eater.'

The bronco screwed his face up in a mask of hatred. He moved forward with blinding speed but Lew managed to parry the thrust with his hatchet. They started to circle each other, looking for a weakness, any advantage that could be exploited.

Back and forth they moved with sure, light-footedness. The bronco made another thrust at Lew's middle, which the scout parried once more. While the knife blade was locked with the head of the hatchet, Lew blurred in and looped a left fist that crashed into the side of the Indian's head. The Apache staggered back, shook his head and doggedly readied himself for another attack.

Both men were sweating profusely as they began their deadly dance once again. The bronco's sinewy torso rippled with every movement he made. Again, he came, in a display of unrelenting pressure. The blade sliced the fabric of Lew's shirt across his middle. He felt a slight burning sensation as the razor-edge scored the skin. The Apache smiled faintly at Lew's wince.

'*Demasiado lento*, Buffalo-Man,' the bronco spat in Spanish. 'Too slow, Buffalo-man.'

Lew set his jaw firmly and moved forward. He swiped swiftly left and right with the hatchet, making the bronco leap out of the deadly weapon's path.

The Apache circled to the left and lunged forward in a surprisingly swift move. It caused Lew to lurch backward to avoid the blow. As that happened, he lost balance and was in motion when he stumbled over a small rock and landed flat on his back.

The Apache's eyes lit up with expectation, and without hesitation he launched himself in a headlong dive at the vulnerable scout.

Lew rolled to his left and the bronco landed on the ground with a dull thud. With barely a pause, Lew brought his hatchet-filled right hand sweeping back in a powerful arc. The honed head buried itself in the Apache's back. The bronco shrieked in pain and his back arched in a violent spasm. He screamed once more when Lew ripped the hatchet free from the ghastly wound. With every ounce of strength that he could muster, he brought it back down at the base of the Apache's head, killing him instantly.

Eden remained there for a few moments while he gathered himself, the sound of his breathing loud in his ears. He looked into the eyes of the dead Indian and sighed, grateful to still be alive.

Then a sudden eruption of gunfire from the Anderson place signaled the start of another attack.

8

'We just lost Shard,' Shannon called from his position at the front window. He stared at the dead soldier who lay near the water trough out in the yard. He had an arrow sticking from his chest.

Carr raised his Springfield carbine and fired a shot at a hidden enemy. The bullet smashed into a large rock the bronco was hiding behind and sent slivers slicing through the air.

'How's that leg of yours, sergeant?'

'Hurts like a bitch,' Shannon growled. 'Now keep shootin'.'

Outside, Murphy had taken up his position once more behind the wagon. He fired a couple of shots and as he reloaded, he looked at the men who were still in the fight. If help didn't arrive soon there was a good chance they'd all be killed.

He wasn't sure how many casualties the broncos had sustained from this attack. There were at least two that he knew of. But he had lost two men, as well. He was the only man left unscathed from the patrol.

He decided that it was time to get everyone who was left inside, where they had more cover.

He called across the yard to Baranski, 'Fall back inside! Fall back!'

The Ukrainian signaled that he'd heard and, keeping low, turned and headed for the doorway of the homestead. He was followed by the remaining few. Only then did he follow the others inside.

Once inside, he made his way to the window where Shannon had placed himself.

'Welcome to the Alamo,' said Shannon.

'There can't be many of them left,' said Murphy. 'We just need to hold out until help arrives.'

Shannon nodded and held out his

hand. It held three bullets. 'That'll be fine — if we don't run out of ammunition first.'

'Therein lies the problem,' Murphy stated with frustration. 'How's Hackett doin'?'

'Carr, is the major still alive?' Shannon called out.

Carr pulled back from the window just as a bullet cracked into the frame. 'He was, the last time I checked.'

'He managed to put him back together,' Shannon explained to Murphy. 'All we have to do now is wait and see. Although it may not matter before too long.'

'How are the women holdin' up?'

Shannon shrugged. 'Okay, I guess. They found out that the son was killed out there. The father and the other son seem to be doin' fine.'

'Hey, look at this,' Baranski called from the window that Carr had just vacated. A line of dried blood ran down the side of the big Ukrainian's face.

Murphy walked over to the window.

'Up on the rise,' Baranski pointed out.

Murphy looked but saw nothing. He was about to walk away when he saw it. A flash. A reflection of sunlight from something bright. It stopped briefly then came again.

'Did you see that, Mordecai?' Murphy asked Shannon.

'I saw it.'

'What do you think?'

'I think Kelso's arrived.'

★   ★   ★

Kelso had indeed arrived. When he saw the detail of blue-clad soldiers appear, Lew breathed a sigh of relief. He'd been in the process of working out a suicidal plan to try and save the remaining people at the Anderson spread. Now it looked as if he could think again.

But he frowned as the column reached him and came to a halt. There was no stage, and no sign of the major's daughter.

When Kelso dismounted, he hurried across and said, 'Report, Lew.'

'It's bad, cap'n,' Lew replied. 'There ain't many of them left that I can figure, and I 'spect they're runnin' low on ammunition. I saw Seamus Murphy, which means that Reardon's patrol is down there, but from what I can tell, there ain't nowhere near enough men for that. Plus, there ain't no sign of the lieutenant.'

Kelso nodded. 'Did you see Sergeant Shannon?'

'Nope. He could be holed up inside, but you know him. He'd rather be front and center than hidin' away from it all.'

'What about the Apaches?'

'That's the puzzle,' Lew replied with a frown. 'There ain't many of them left, either. I'd have thought they would've given up by now. But they just keep at them. It's like they just want to get inside that homestead.'

While that sunk in, he asked, 'The stagecoach?'

'The Mimbreños hit Adler Springs before we got there,' Kelso explained. 'It looks like they chased the stage in. They killed everyone except for Major Hackett's daughter. I think they took her with them.'

Lew digested the news in silence.

'Now,' said Kelso, 'let's go finish those Apaches.'

Minutes later, after signaling the homestead with a piece of broken mirror, Company 'C' was mounted line abreast and ready to proceed.

Kelso drew his sidearm and raised it into the air. '*Company 'C'! Charge!*'

They came over the rise, a thundering line of horsemen yelling wildly. The hidden broncos leaped from their cover. They fired a couple of shots and then started to retreat. Gunfire erupted from the homestead and both forces caught the retreating Apaches in the open. Kelso saw two go down in a mass of flailing arms and legs.

Beaten and knowing it, the survivors threw down their weapons and raised their hands in the air. There were just three of them still standing.

Hauling back on his reins, Kelso shouted, '*Cease fire! Cease fire!*'

The echoes of the gunfire died away as three of Kelso's men moved to take the remaining Apaches prisoner. In the meantime, Seamus Murphy emerged from the ranch house, followed by Baranski. Limping along behind them came Shannon, a bloodstained bandage wrapped around the wound on his leg.

Kelso dismounted and walked over to them.

'It's good to see you, cap'n,' Murphy greeted him. 'It was lookin' a little grim until you showed.'

'I'm sorry I couldn't get here sooner,' said Kelso. 'Sergeant Shannon, you're wounded I see.'

'It ain't much, sir.'

'How's Major Hackett?'

'He's still alive, sir, for now.'

Kelso looked around the yard.

'Where's your patrol, Seamus?'

Murphy gave him a pained look. 'Inside, sor. What's left of them. Along with the lieutenant.'

He went on to explain about the ambush.

'I was afraid something like that would happen,' Kelso allowed. 'What about your men, sergeant?'

'The company lost two men, sir,' Shannon informed him. 'Morse and Edwards.'

'That's three. All good men.'

As Lew strode up, Kelso asked, 'Is Beshe with the survivors, Lew?'

'Yes, cap'n,' the scout confirmed. 'I've only seen him the once, but it's him alright.'

'Good. I'll see him in a moment, after I've checked on Major Hackett.'

He was about to go inside when a hand on his arm stayed him. Looking back at Lew, Kelso frowned.

'There sir, the girl,' Lew explained in a low voice.

Kelso, Shannon and Murphy turned

and looked at Muriel Anderson, who'd come outside into the sun.

'What about her?' asked Kelso.

'Look at her.'

'I am,' Kelso said, a slight edge to his voice.

'No, cap'n. I mean *really* look at her.'

Kelso let his gaze linger on the young lady for a while before he saw it. She had long, lustrous black hair, olive skin, a slim build, and high cheekbones. He guessed she would be around sixteen-years-old. He turned his eyes to look at the scout. Lew saw the recognition in Kelso's eyes.

'I think we've found the reason the Apaches were so persistent,' he observed.

'I agree. Let's have a word with Mrs. Anderson.'

★　★　★

Betty Anderson wiped at the tears as they rolled down her red cheeks. Her brown eyes glistened with moisture.

'How did you figure it out?'

'I didn't,' Kelso admitted. 'It was Lew Eden here who did that.'

She let her eyes flick toward Lew and then back. She nodded. 'What you say is true. Muriel *is* half Apache.'

'Who's her father?'

Betty hesitated before saying, 'Beshe.'

'So, he was here to get her?'

She nodded. 'Please don't say anything in front of Muriel. To her, John is her father. He's the only one she's ever known. If she ever found out . . . '

'Do you mind telling me about it?' Kelso asked.

'It all happened a lifetime ago. I was on a stage bound for Tucson. The Apaches hit it in the middle of nowhere. Everyone on it was killed, except me. They took me captive for six months. I managed to escape, but not before Beshe took me for his wife. When I managed to get away, I was already five months pregnant.'

Betty paused to gather herself before continuing. 'John found me three days later, wandering around the desert. He cared for me until I got better. One thing led to another and I never left. He was living near Phoenix at the time. He already had the two boys. Their mother had died the previous year, so it suited both of us. And after Muriel was born, he loved her and treated her as though she was his.'

'They must have been on their way here when the patrol was ambushed,' Murphy said.

'But they've been tearin' up the territory for weeks,' Shannon pointed out.

'That's because they didn't know where the Andersons lived,' Lew guessed. He looked at Betty. 'Do you happen to know an old prospector by the name of Soapy Smith, by any chance?'

'Why, yes,' Betty said. 'He comes here quite often.'

Lew glanced at Kelso, who nodded. 'It doesn't explain why they followed you.'

The scout shrugged. 'Maybe they just wanted me dead because I'd been trailin' them. Who knows why they do what they do.'

'Mrs. Anderson, it might pay for you all to come into Ocotillo Creek for a while. At least until your husband and son are better,' Kelso suggested.

She looked about the room at the wounded who lay anywhere there was space. 'No. We'll be fine. I can take care of them here. I don't wish to be chased from my own home. Really,' she reiterated, 'we'll be fine.'

'Well . . . if your mind's set. But please, at least think about it.'

Betty Anderson turned and left the men to talk.

'Once we get back to the fort, Mordecai, you're relieved of duty until your leg gets better.'

Shannon opened his mouth to protest, but decided against it when he saw the firm set of Kelso's mouth. Instead, he asked, 'Are you goin' after the girl?'

'Eventually, yes,' Kelso acknowledged.

'You'll need a top-kick. Can I name my replacement?'

Kelso surprised him by saying, 'By all means.'

'Take Seamus with you, sir.'

'What do you say, Seamus?' Kelso asked.

'I'll go, sor,' the Irishman acknowledged.

'Good. That'll be all for the moment. Lew, can I have a word?'

When Shannon and Murphy had gone, Kelso said, 'I want to send you out to look for the Mimbreños. It looks as though they're headed for the Santa Rita Mountains.'

'Good place to hole up,' Lew acknowledged.

'Can you get there and back in a week?'

'And find the Apaches?'

'That's the idea.'

'No guarantees, but I'll do my best.'

'Good. Take whatever you need and

go. We'll be ready to ride when you return.'

'You know there's a good chance she's already dead, don't you?' Lew pointed out.

Kelso nodded. 'There's that possibility. But I'm thinking that if they wanted to kill her, then they would have done it at Adler Springs. Just maybe they have something else in store for her.'

'I sure hope you're right, cap'n.'

'Excuse me, cap'n?'

Kelso turned to see Carr standing there. 'I believe you managed to save the major's life,' he said. 'All that training must have paid off.'

'He's not out of the woods yet, sir.'

'Still, if it weren't for you, he'd be dead by now. Anyway, what can I do for you?'

'Major Hackett is awake and asking for you.'

Kelso blinked, surprised by the news. 'I'll be right along.' He turned his attention back to his scout. 'Find the

Apaches, Lew. And find that girl.'
'Yes, cap'n. I'll do what I can.'

9

In the dull light of the homestead, Major Matthew Hackett looked more dead than alive. His face was gaunt, his eyes were sunken and dull and the bandage swathed around his head was stained with blood. He seemed alert, but when he spoke, his voice was almost inaudible.

'Where's . . . Amelia?' he managed in a hoarse whisper.

'Get some rest, sir,' Kelso said, deflecting the question. 'We'll talk about it later.'

With considerable effort, he grasped at Kelso's arm. 'Where?'

'The Apaches got to Adler Springs before we did,' Kelso explained. 'They killed everyone there, except for Amelia. They took her with them. I've just sent Lew out to find them.'

He could see the pain in Hackett's

eyes as the news sank in. Then the pain was replaced by anger as they found Kelso's face.

'This is your fault,' he hissed. 'You were drinking again, weren't you? You were late because you were drinking. And because of that, you've cost me . . . my daughter!'

Hackett's hand fell away and he gasped for breath. Kelso was stunned at the accusation. He opened his mouth to protest, but it was no use. The effort had sapped all the strength from his commanding officer, and Hackett had lapsed back into unconsciousness.

Kelso looked across at Carr, who had witnessed the entire exchange. 'Can he be taken back to Whitethorn?'

'If you can find a way to transport him layin' down, sir.'

'You can use our wagon,' Betty Anderson interjected.

'Thank you, ma'am, I appreciate it.'

Kelso went outside to find Murphy.

'Seamus, hitch a team up to the Anderson's wagon. We'll be using it to transport the wounded back to Whitethorn.'

'I'll see to it, cap'n.'

Mordecai Shannon came up behind Kelso and asked, 'Are we leavin'?'

'Soon,' Kelso informed him. He looked Shannon in the eye and said, 'The major believes it was my fault that his daughter was taken. What do *you* think?'

'It don't matter much *what* I think,' Shannon replied. 'What I know is that if you and the others hadn't turned up when you did, we'd have run out of ammunition, and that would have been it for us.'

Kelso nodded. 'All right. If you can manage it, give Seamus a hand.'

'Sir.'

★ ★ ★

Two days after leaving the Anderson spread, a line of weary, dust-covered soldiers rode through the gates at Fort Whitethorn. The wounded were on the wagon while the Apache prisoners rode horses tied together at the rear of the column.

As he dismounted, Kelso was met by Captain Dawson Bragg. A slim-built twenty-three-year-old with black hair and brown eyes, Bragg's uncle was Brigadier General Edward S. Bragg, one-time commander of the Iron Brigade and now a member of Congress. The captain's family had used the general's standing to have their son accepted into West Point, and then posted to Whitethorn, where he could get field command experience. It was something that hadn't gone unnoticed by Whitethorn's commanding officer, who also had designs on entering politics before he turned fifty.

Bragg had been looking over the bone-tired column while Kelso dismounted, then asked abruptly, 'What the hell happened?'

Kelso was about to fire back a rebuke but weariness overcame him and he let it pass. 'Didn't the rider I sent ahead explain it?'

'He did. But why did you split your force? You *never* split it. We were taught that at West Point after the Custer fiasco.'

This time Kelso's surge of anger wouldn't be stopped. 'This isn't West Point, Bragg, and I'm not Custer. And if you'd listened to what the man I sent ahead had to say, you'd understand that splitting my force was my only option. Now get the hell away from me!'

'How dare — '

Eyes blazing, Kelso snarled, 'Listen, you jumped up little ass — I don't care who you are or what our commanding officer thinks of you. I'm still senior to you, so when you talk to me, you show some damned respect! Now go away!'

Bragg stormed off and left Kelso standing beside his horse, his hands trembling with rage. The captain looked about to see if any of the men had overheard the exchange. Immediately his gaze locked on that of Shannon and he caught a glimpse of something he never expected to see in his lifetime — respect.

'Sergeant Shannon?'

'Sir?'

'After you've had that leg of yours seen to by Doc Sutton, and if you're able, I'd like to see you and Sergeant Murphy.'

'Yes, sir.'

'Sergeant Murphy?'

'Cap'n?'

Kelso turned to look at the Irishman. 'See to the men.'

'Sir.'

'And Seamus?'

'Yes, sor?'

'Welcome to Company 'C'.'

★ ★ ★

An hour later, Kelso was summoned to the post infirmary. Upon entry, he found Bragg standing beside Matthew Hackett's bedside.

'Good, you're . . . here,' Hackett said weakly.

'I came as soon as the orderly found me, sir.'

'As you know, I'm . . . going to be laid up . . . ' Hackett paused a moment before continuing. 'I'm going to be laid up for . . . quite a while. I'm placing Bragg in command of Whitethorn.'

Kelso couldn't disguise the look of alarm that flitted across his face. When he saw the smug expression on Bragg's face, that alarm quickly turned to anger.

'And before you ask . . . why, you should already know . . . the answer,' Hackett explained.

'As senior officer, sir, that responsibility should be mine,' Kelso pointed out anyway.

'The major has made his decision,' Bragg said in a condescending tone.

Before he could stop himself, Kelso blurted out. 'Shut up, Bragg. You know I'm right. And so does the major.'

Bragg's face turned red as his rage boiled.

'I've made my . . . decision, captain,' Hackett hissed. 'Once I'm fit enough, you will . . . face a court martial.'

'*What?*' Kelso asked incredulously.

'Dereliction of . . . duty.'

'It'll have to wait until I return,' Kelso said defiantly.

'Where do you think you're going,' Bragg demanded.

'As soon as Lew Eden returns, I'm taking the company out after the major's daughter.'

'The hell you are,' Bragg snapped. 'You'll take them nowhere.'

Fixing his eyes on Hackett, Kelso said, 'Major?'

'You'll stay . . . on this post, captain,' Hackett ordered. 'If anyone goes out . . . after my daughter, it will be one of the other . . . officers.'

The captain looked at the cot beside that of his commanding officer. Then he brought his gaze back to Hackett and protested. 'And have them end up like Reardon's patrol? You damn well know that the only hope your daughter has rests with me and my men.'

'I have spoken, damn it!' Hackett shouted hoarsely, before breaking into a fit of coughing.

Kelso looked at both men defiantly and announced, 'Then you'll have to court martial me for disobeying orders, major, because I'm damned well going anyway!'

With that, Kelso turned on his heel and stalked out.

Once outside, he paused under the awning, breathing deeply as he tried to bring his temper in check. Damn them!

'Cap'n?'

Kelso turned to his left and saw Shannon and Murphy approaching. Both wore clean uniforms after changing from the bloodstained, torn and dust-covered ones they'd worn for the previous few days.

'Good, you're here,' Kelso said. 'My quarters. Now!'

'So, there you have it,' Kelso finished. 'Bragg is the new commanding officer of Whitethorn, and I'm to be court-martialed.'

'It's horseshit, sir.'

All eyes settled on Mordecai Shannon. Kelso never thought the sergeant would show his support. In fact, he wouldn't have been surprised if he'd said, 'I told you so'.

'Sergeant?'

'I'm sorry, sir, but it is,' Shannon explained. 'I know we don't see eye to eye, but having you court-martialed for dereliction of duty isn't right. Not for that. And to place Bragg, whose only concern is for himself, in charge of the fort, that ain't right either.'

'What are we goin' to do, cap'n?' Murphy asked.

'We'll wait for Lew to return,' Kelso said. 'Then I'm taking 'C' out to find the major's daughter.'

'I'm not sure if that's wise, sir,'

Shannon warned.

'Let them add it to my charge sheet.'

Shannon and Murphy looked at each other before the former spoke, 'What do you need us to do?'

'Are you sure?'

'Yes, sir.'

'Right — first off, we're going to need four replacements for the wounded men and those we lost.'

'Since we have Seamus, sir, we'll only need another three,' Shannon pointed out.

'You're on the list of wounded, Sergeant,' Kelso reminded him.

'No, I ain't,' Shannon told him.

'I can't have you along with that leg of yours.'

'The hell you can't! It ain't like we're walkin' there, is it?'

Against his better judgment, Kelso said, 'I'll give you until Eden gets back. And if I judge you aren't fit enough, you stay.'

'Fair enough.'

'Now, do you have any ideas as to

who we can obtain as replacements?'

'How about Willard Roberson?' Murphy suggested. Roberson was a soldier with a past no one knew much about. Word was, he had once been an outlaw who joined up to escape the law. That said, he was one hell of a good soldier, and could blow a bugle as good as the next man, which might come in handy.

'He's in,' said Kelso.

'What about Michael Flannery?' Murphy suggested.

'That's all we need, another hard-headed Mick,' Shannon muttered.

'Is that an objection, sergeant?' Kelso asked.

'No, sir. Flannery will fight. I've no doubt about that. His problem is knowin' when to stop.'

'Well, God knows we need fighters right now. All right — he's in, too. That leaves one more.'

'Cass,' Shannon said, emphatically.

Kelso and Murphy stared at him in silence. Cass was short for Cassadore, another of the scouts employed at Whitethorn.

'He's a Mescalero,' Kelso pointed out.

'He's a good man, sir. We can use him. Besides, it can't hurt. Even General Crook uses them, as you well know. What about 'Peaches'?'

Peaches was the bastardized name for Crook's personal scout — bastardized because no one could pronounce his real name, which was Panayatishn.

'Point taken. Any objections Seamus?'

'No, sir. I've worked with him before. He'll do.'

'Right then, see to it.'

'What will we say if we're asked about the new men, sor?' Murphy inquired.

'Just replacements, Seamus. That's all they are.'

'Yes, sor.'

After they were gone, the first thing that entered Kelso's mind was, *I need a drink.*

He crossed to the trunk where he kept the bottles. He opened the lid and reached in. After pulling the cork, Kelso lifted it to his lips. The smell of cheap whiskey flooded his nostrils and he paused. Then it all became too much, and he drank.

10

The Santa Rita Mountains — later renamed the Sky Island Mountain Range — was an isolated range surrounded by country that differed vastly to the oak-pine vegetation on the lower slopes, and pine forests higher up. Yet it was common to find desert plants such as yucca and agaves there, too. It had rugged, steep slopes with sharp peaks and narrow ridges, and played home to big cats like jaguar, bobcat, and mountain lion, not to mention black bear, turkey, white-tailed and mule deer.

In short, it was a haven where the Mimbreños could retreat with relative safety, with plentiful food and water.

Above the pine forest, Lew Eden saw an eagle circling lazily. He drew his paint horse to a halt and unhooked the canteen from his saddle. Lew had been following a rough trail with small, half-buried rocks scattered along it.

For two days he'd been scouring the area, looking for sign of the Mimbreños and where they might be holed up, but so far he'd found nothing.

He looked up at the eagle again just in time to see it start to dive. Down it came, eyes locked onto its unsuspecting target. Then it stopped mid-dive and cut to the left, screeching its frustration. Someone was coming along the trail behind him.

Alarm ran through the scout. Without a second thought, he pulled the paint off the trail and into a dense stand of trees. There he waited patiently. Two minutes turned to three. After five had passed, they appeared. Four Mimbreño Apaches, riding quietly along the trail that Lew had just vacated.

The scout leaned forward in his saddle and rubbed at the paint's neck to keep it quiet. They rode slowly past his position. One of them had a white-tailed deer draped across his lap.

A hunting party, Lew concluded. At least now he would be able to follow them to their main camp.

For the next two hours, he shadowed from a safe distance until they approached a steep granite-faced escarpment. They skirted around the base until the trail narrowed to a twisting path that climbed toward the top.

Lew watched them from a stand of pines. He was certain their camp was at the end of the rough trail they were now traversing. He was also certain there would be a lookout somewhere near the top.

The Mimbreños stopped as they neared the summit, and the leader raised his hand above his head. After a few moments, the lookout appeared and answered the signal with one of his own. Then the hunting party moved on and out of sight.

They had chosen a highly defensible place for their stronghold. The approach could be observed easily and the fore-warned Apaches could concentrate their numbers to cover the rugged trail. Anyone climbing towards the top would be strung out due to the narrow path, then exposed to a withering hail of gunfire.

There had to be another way.

After another two hours of careful searching, Lew found it. And it wasn't good.

*   *   *

The harsh morning sunlight stabbed Kelso in the eye as he stepped from his dimly lit quarters. His head hurt, his mouth tasted like a horse had shat in it, and his guts crawled inside. He fought down the urge to empty its contents all over his boots and walked out onto the parade ground.

Somewhere a bugle blared and the brassy sound almost made his head explode. Kelso cursed under his breath and massaged his throbbing temples.

'Excuse me, cap'n.'

Kelso turned to look at Shannon. 'What is it, sergeant?'

Shannon stared at Kelso for a moment and the captain could see that any respect he'd built with the sergeant instantly evaporated.

'There's somethin' for you over at the stables.'

Kelso nodded. 'What?'

'It's a crate, sir. I've no idea what's in it.'

Through the fog inside his head, Kelso thought for a time then smiled, despite the throbbing.

'Come with me,' he ordered Shannon.

The sergeant had to hurry to keep up with his commanding officer as they crossed the parade ground. Once in the stables, the pungent odor of straw, horse sweat and manure assailed their nostrils. Without having to be shown, Kelso found what he was looking for and prised the lid free.

Shannon watched as he reached inside and took out a tomahawk. But not just any tomahawk. It might have looked plain, with no markings or adornments of any kind, but it was perfectly balanced for throwing, and razor sharp.

Kelso held it up and looked at Shannon. 'I ordered these after the first mission. Every man in Company 'C' is to have one.'

Shannon couldn't help but raise his eyebrows. 'Major Hackett let you order a shipment of non-regulation weapons?'

Shaking his head Kelso said, 'He didn't. I did it myself. The money was my own.'

The sergeant stared at Kelso, unsure of what to make of the captain's revelation. On one hand, Kelso had slipped back into old habits as soon as he'd reached the fort. On the other, here was a man so dedicated to his company that he used his own money to provide them with weapons.

'I figured Lew could train everyone on how to use them. I also figure they will be a sight more useful up close than a knife,' Kelso explained.

'Permission to speak freely, sir?'

Kelso nodded.

'I'm damned if I can figure you out,' Shannon said. 'You have the ability to be one of the best officers I've ever served, and yet you're a damned drunk. When we came back from the last patrol, I thought that maybe you were goin' to start livin' up to that potential. But then you fell straight back into the bottle. I know the major overlooking you for command of Whitethorn must have been a kick in the guts, but can you blame him? We've all been kicked before, and we keep gettin' back up. You get kicked and you run straight for a bottle of whiskey.'

Kelso could feel his anger rising and opened his mouth to speak. Shannon, however, wasn't finished, and was determined to voice his opinion at length.

'You just shut up and listen, cap'n. If you keep goin' the way you are, you'll get every man in Company 'C' killed, includin' yourself. I was goin' to tell you this mornin' that I wanted out before you did that. But this . . . ' he pointed at the crate, 'This has got me thinkin' about givin' you one final chance. Seamus Murphy said you were a good officer. Now's your chance to show us all if you are or not.'

Kelso glared at Shannon in silence. He restrained himself and said, simply, 'Are you finished?'

'Sir,' Shannon snapped.

'You seem to forget that I am to be court-martialed.'

'Not anytime soon, sir.'

'See that all the men, including yourself, get one of these,' he said, handing him the tomahawk.

'Yes, sir.'

Kelso was about to leave him to it when Bragg and two other soldiers entered the stables.

'There he is,' Bragg said, pointing at Kelso.

Out of the corner of his eye, Kelso saw Shannon place the tomahawk into the crate and replace the lid.

'You're under arrest, Captain Kelso,' Bragg stated.

'I'm *what?*'

'I said, you're under arrest. These men will escort you to the guardhouse.'

'On what charge?'

'For disobeying orders.'

'What damned orders?' Kelso snapped.

'Sir!'

'*What?*'

'You will address me as sir,' Bragg ordered.

'The hell I will,' Kelso snarled. 'What damned orders?'

'It has been brought to my attention that you are organizing to take your so-called 'Company' out on patrol when you were specifically ordered not to.'

'Are you arresting me for something that I *might* do?' Kelso asked incredulously.

'You can't do that, sir,' Shannon said.

'You shall remain silent, sergeant. If I want you to speak I shall tell you to,'

Bragg said coldly.

Shannon bit back a retort, but not Kelso. He was livid and wanted this entitled maggot to feel the force of his pent-up rage and frustration.

'You listen to me, you spoon-fed son of a bitch. You may be in overall charge of the fort, but I'm still senior. So, you'll show some respect!'

'You're right,' Bragg sneered. 'I'm in charge. Take him away and lock him up.'

With one man either side of him, Kelso was marched to the guardhouse.

* * *

Lew Eden had watched the Mimbreño camp for most of the day, hoping to get a glimpse of Amelia Hackett. What he got was more than he bargained for. The stronghold contained not just one, but four white women.

The scout had moved in on the camp during the night. It had been an arduous task and it had taken a

137

significant amount of time. Come dawn he was hidden amongst rocks and pines overlooking the camp. He figured there to be thirty warriors down there, a little less than the forty Lew had expected.

From his position, he could see that everything, including the entry to the stronghold and his assumption, was right. There was only one way in by horseback — a route which spelled certain death to an attacking force.

It also explained why the white captives were allowed to walk about unguarded. After all, there was nowhere for them to go. A rough wickiup had been built for them to shelter in, which confused Lew because Apaches would never normally worry about their captives' comfort.

A sudden rifle shot shattered the tranquility of the afternoon and a shout echoed throughout the camp. Apaches scrambled about the stronghold, taking up guarded positions. A group of riders came into view. Three were Mimbreño and two were white men.

They stopped in the middle of the camp and dismounted. There was a brief discussion, after which the captives were lined up and looked over by the newcomers.

'Slavers,' Lew grumbled in disgust.

Following the inspection, the women were herded away and the Apaches and white men settled down to talk business. The conversation lasted around twenty minutes before negotiations finished. The two white men climbed back on their horses and were escorted away by the warriors who'd brought them in.

Their arrival cast a new light over the problem and Lew knew he had to get back to Whitethorn as fast as possible . . . and hope that Company 'C' could get back quickly enough to rescue the women before they disappeared.

11

Amelia Hackett was scared witless and bone tired. The events of the past few days had sapped all of her energy and all she wanted was to lay down and never get back up. The arrival of the two white men had put paid to that idea, and all she could think of now was whether or not she would ever see her father again.

She sat her thin frame down on a large rock and rubbed at her shoulder-length, matted black hair. The horrors of the day the Mimbreños had taken her were still raw in her mind. At first, Amelia thought that she would die horribly like the others. In her mind, she could still hear the screams of the dying. But the Apaches had kept her alive, and now she knew why. She was to be sold to the white men for rifles. Her and the others.

For two and a half days they had traveled through the desert, Amelia atop a mount the Apaches had issued her with. Her hands were tied tightly and her leather bonds bit deeply into her skin. The sun was unrelenting and her pale skin was now sun burnt and filthy.

The war party had come off the desert and climbed into the mountains through oak and pine until they finally reached their destination. Upon her arrival, Amelia found she wasn't the only white captive. There were three others, all younger women like her, and none over twenty.

Their names were Pattie, Elmira, and Maria. Pattie came from a small ranch over near the Arizona border. All of her family had been killed in the raid. Elmira was the daughter of a home-steader. Again, all were killed. And Maria was the daughter of a wealthy Mexican rancho owner. The Apaches had picked her up just before crossing the border.

'Where do you think they'll take us?' blonde-headed Elmira asked.

'New Orleans,' Pattie said. 'I heard one of them say.'

'Why would they take us there?'

'Plenty of money and plenty of men with needs,' Pattie said.

'What do you mean?' Amelia asked, joining the conversation.

'You mean you don't *know?*' Pattie asked soberly.

'No,' Amelia said, shaking her head.

'Sweetie, when them fellers take us back to New Orleans, we'll be lost in the darkest depths that the city has to offer. We'll be sold on to gentlemen's clubs, whore houses, and other bawdy places from which there will be no escape. They'll own us until the day we die.'

A hand flew to Amelia's mouth. 'Surely not.'

'The sooner you accept it, the better off you'll be,' Pattie told her. 'Face it, the life you knew is as dead and gone as my family. You have two choices, live or die.'

'That's enough,' Elmira said, blue eyes flashing with anger. 'We get the picture. There's no need to go on about it.'

Pattie shrugged. 'I'm just tellin' it how it is.'

'Then how about you shut up,' Elmira hissed.

★ ★ ★

For six days, Kelso was locked in the guardhouse awaiting his court martial. Although he didn't want to admit it, it had done him some good. Six whole days without a drink. Even the shakes were gone. He still wanted to kill Bragg, but he certainly felt clearer in the head. Be damned if he felt any gratitude towards the little upstart.

A key rattled in the door lock and as it swung open, the hinges protested with a loud screech. Two men stepped into the small cell. 'The cap'n wants to see you.'

'What about?' Kelso asked.

'He didn't say.'

'Tell him if he wants to see me, he knows where to find me.'

'The cap'n said to bring you with us, sir. He also said that we could shoot you if you acted uppity.'

'And would you do that?'

Both men shook their heads. 'No, sir.'

'All right, then, let's go and see what he wants.'

Both soldiers gave out a sigh of relief. 'After you, sir.'

They walked outside into the harsh glare of the afternoon sun. The heat was almost suffocating, and Kelso realized how cool the guardhouse was throughout blistering hot days and felt grateful for that, at least.

Halfway across to headquarters, a dust-covered rider on a tired paint horse rode in through the fort's gates.

Kelso stopped and said, 'Wait up.'

All three stopped in the middle of the parade ground and waited. Lew spotted them and angled his horse over to where they stood. He looked as tired as his horse. He dismounted and slapped some of the dust from his clothes.

'It's good to see you, Lew,' Kelso greeted. 'Do you have news?'

'Sure do, cap'n,' Lew croaked, his throat dry. 'I found 'em. But they ain't goin' to be there for much longer.'

'How do you mean?'

'While I was there watchin' the camp, a couple of fellers turned up. Escorted into the stronghold they was,' Lew explained.

'Where *is* this stronghold of theirs?'

'In the Santa Ritas, like you thought. But like I said, they ain't goin' to be there for long. Them couple of fellers were slavers. They'll be back soon to take them women outta there quick smart.'

Kelso raised his eyebrows. 'Women?'

'There's four of 'em, cap'n.'

'Can the company get in there, Lew?'

'There's one way in and out,' Eden explained. 'The Mimbreños have a clear field of fire across the approach and whoever tries to get in that way'll get slaughtered, no two ways about it.'

'Then how do we get in?'

'Sir?' one of Kelso's escorts said hesitantly.

Lew looked at them, and for the first time realized that something was wrong.

'What's goin' on?' his voice rumbled.

Kelso avoided the question. 'Go see Shannon and tell him what you found. Then get yourself some food and some sleep.'

Lew stared pointedly at Kelso and asked, 'Have you been drinkin'?'

Kelso smiled at him. 'Not for the past six days. Go and find Mordecai. He'll fill you in.'

Lew watched the small party trek towards the headquarters building and shook his head, wondering if everything had finally caught up with Captain Nathan Kelso.

⋆ ⋆ ⋆

'It's about time you lot arrived,' Bragg snapped. 'It isn't like you had to go to

146

Mexico to bring him back. Next time I ask you to do something, make it faster.'

The office was hot and stuffy, the enclosed air rank with the smell of Bragg's sour sweat.

'What do you want, Bragg?' Kelso asked impatiently.

'That's *Captain* Bragg to you.'

'Are you really goin' to do this?'

'You need to learn respect, Captain Kelso,' Bragg said, arrogance dripping from his voice. 'For both your uniform and your betters.'

Kelso shook his head. 'Just get on with it. It's too damned hot to be standing around swapping nonsense with you.'

Bragg pushed a sheet of paper across his desk. 'This piece of paper could save you, and us, the trouble of a court-martial. All you have to do is sign it.'

Kelso scooped it up from the battered desktop. 'What the hell is it?'

He read it through and looked up at

Bragg. He glared at the smug looking captain then did the last thing that Bragg expected. He tore the sheet of paper up. His opposite number's face dropped.

'What do you think you're doing?' he blustered. 'That was your way out!'

'And what would happen to Company 'C' if I just rolled over and did nothing?'

'I would take . . . They would get a new commanding officer,' Bragg corrected.

'So, that's it,' Kelso accused. 'You want my command. You see it as a quick trip to the top. Win a few battles and heap glory upon yourself at the expense of others. Well, let me tell you something. You don't win battles by getting all your men killed. Custer learned that — the hard way.'

'I'll not be spoken to like that!' Bragg barked. 'Remember, I'm still in command of the fort.'

'Well then, command!' Kelso snarled. 'Lew Eden just rode back into Whitethorn with news of the Mimbreños and their captives.'

'You mean Amelia Hackett?'

'Not just her. Lew said there were four women at the stronghold. Four. But they won't be there for long. While he was there, slavers turned up and then left. He figures they'll be back soon to close whatever deal they made and take them away. I suggest you let me take my men and get them the hell out of there before that happens.'

'Where *is* Eden?'

'He was going to see Sergeant Shannon and then going to get something to eat.'

Bragg looked at one of the two guards. 'Get Eden. Let's hear what he has to say.'

* * *

Lew was followed into the office by Shannon. They stood in front of the desk and waited for Bragg to speak.

'Right, Eden. Tell me what it is that

you saw out there, then tell me why you didn't report it directly to your commanding officer.'

'I did. I reported it to the cap'n here,' Lew said.

'But you should have come to *me*, your commanding officer,' Bragg said in a stern voice.

'Just so you know, cap'n, you ain't *my* commanding officer,' Lew rumbled.

Bragg's face colored and his jaw firmed. However, he decided not to push it. 'Tell me what you saw.'

When Lew had finished, Bragg asked, 'Is there another way in?'

'It'll be tough, but it can be done.'

'Well?' Bragg asked impatiently.

'Around back of the stronghold, there's a steep rock-face. It was the way I was able to get in unseen.'

'How would fifteen men go climbing it?' Bragg asked.

'It would be impossible for them to do it in the daylight without being seen.'

'*You* did it,' Bragg pointed out.

Lew nodded. 'I was one man — and not loaded down by all the equipment you soldier-boys usually carry with you.'

'Then what would you suggest?'

'That it be done at night,' Lew told him. 'The other way is too dangerous.'

Bragg raised his eyebrows. 'Fifteen men carrying weapons climb it at night?'

Even Kelso didn't like the idea, but he kept his face passive. Bragg looked at him.

'You claim that these men of yours are the best Fort Whitethorn has to offer, do you not?'

'I don't claim it,' Kelso replied. 'They *are*.'

'Then they should be able to perform a frontal attack and take the Indians' position,' Bragg theorized.

Mordecai Shannon stepped forward, concern etched across his face. 'Sir.'

'I'll not lead my men into a slaughter,' Kelso protested.

'Not you, Kelso, *me*,' Bragg stated.

'I will lead them. You'll be in the guardhouse, awaiting court-martial. We'll leave tomorrow.'

Kelso's face tightened with rage. He took a step forward but a hand from Mordecai Shannon stopped him. 'Captain, you're in enough trouble as it is, without doin' anythin' else.'

The infuriated officer glared at Bragg and hissed, 'If you want to get yourself killed, fine. But don't go getting my men killed with you!'

'They're not yours anymore. Get him out of here. Sergeant Shannon, have Company 'C' ready to leave at sunup.'

'No, sir.'

'I beg your pardon?'

Shannon stared straight ahead. 'I'll not be part of you killin' all of Company 'C' for your own benefit.'

Bragg shook his head in disbelief. 'I'm sorry you feel that way. You can join Kelso in the guardhouse.'

Shannon snapped to attention. 'Sir.'

'Get them the hell out of my sight.'

Once outside, Kelso left his escort

behind and headed straight for the infirmary.

'This way, sir,' one of the escorting soldiers called after him.

Kelso ignored him and kept walking.

'Where are you going?' Lew called after him.

'To see the only man that I might be able to talk some sense into.'

The scout looked at Shannon, who shrugged his shoulders. Then they followed in Kelso's footsteps.

12

Major Hackett was sitting up in his cot, looking a lot better than the last time Kelso had seen him. Gone were the sunken eyes, and color had returned to his gaunt face. His head was still bandaged, but by the looks of him, he was well on his way to making a full recovery.

He looked up as the three men approached his bedside, and his expression grew dark.

'What do you want?' he grunted at Kelso. 'I thought you were safely locked up in the guardhouse.'

'I thought that you would like to know that Lew here has found your daughter,' Kelso told him.

Hackett's eyes lit up and he looked around the room, expecting to see her. 'Where is she? Is she all right?'

'She's in the Santa Rita Mountains,'

Kelso said coldly. 'And she's about to be sold, along with three other women, to white slavers.'

Hackett's mouth opened but no words came out.

'Your golden boy, whom you placed in charge, is planning on taking Company 'C' out tomorrow to mount a rescue effort,' Kelso explained.

'But that's good,' Hackett said eagerly.

'Not the way he intends to do it. He'll get himself and all of my men killed — not to mention your daughter.'

An alarmed expression crossed Hackett's face. His eyes flicked as he thought about what Kelso had just told him. Then his expression changed and he gave Kelso a knowing look.

'This isn't about the hostages or your men,' he stated. 'This is about you being relieved of your command. Not being able to claim the glory for yourself. If you weren't such a drunk . . . '

'I haven't had a drink for almost a

week, damn your eyes!' Kelso snarled. 'And while we're at it, let's get something else straight, too. This isn't about glory or anything like it. This is about Bragg and the power of command having gone to his head! This is about the lives of fifteen men and four women, who'll die if he does what he says he's going to do. Now, I don't give a damn if the son of a bitch gets himself killed, but he isn't taking my men with him — or those women — if I can help it!'

'You're exaggerating,' Hackett scoffed.

Kelso cursed in exasperation. 'Tell him, Lew.'

By the time Lew had finished, the concern was noticeable on Hackett's face. He looked from the scout to Kelso, to Shannon, then back to Kelso.

'You've already had one patrol virtually wiped out,' Kelso pointed out. 'Do you want to lose another?'

'Of course not!' Hackett blustered.

'Then get me and Sergeant Shannon out of the guardhouse so we can go after the Mimbreños and get your daughter back,' Kelso urged.

Hackett glanced at Shannon. 'You in the guardhouse, too? What was your crime?'

'Didn't consider it a crime, sir,' Shannon answered. 'Just didn't fancy dyin' alongside Cap'n Bragg, sir, not bein' a party to getting' them women killed, either.'

'You refused to ride with him,' said Hackett. 'You refused a direct order.'

'The man is a fool, sir.'

'Show some respect, sergeant,' Hackett said curtly.

'Sir.'

Hackett switched his gaze back to Kelso. 'I appreciate your motives, captain. But there's nothing I can do.'

'You mean there's nothing you *will* do,' Kelso accused.

'I mean can't,' Hackett replied. 'You don't understand.'

'Then why don't you explain to me why my men are going to die?'

'Bragg is in command of Fort

Whitethorn. Once I handed it over to him, that was it. I declared myself incapable, and until I'm passed fit, I can do nothing about it. My hands are tied.'

'Get the doctor to pass you.'

'It's not that simple.'

'How long until you *are* passed fit, then?'

'Another five days . . . and by then it'll be too late.'

'Yes, it will.'

A heavy silence descended upon the group.

'There might be another way,' Lew muttered.

'How?' demanded Hackett.

The scout turned to look at the two guards who'd escorted them in. 'Go outside.'

They looked at Hackett. The major nodded and they left the infirmary.

'Well?'

'The cap'n takes the company out tonight under the cover of darkness, while Bragg's asleep.'

'And how do you propose he does that?'

'It's probably best if you don't know that,' Lew replied.

'You *do* realize how much of a hornet's nest this'll stir up, don't you?' Hackett pointed out.

'I figure that it will take two or three days riding to get where the Mimbreños have their stronghold,' Lew explained. 'From there it will be roughly the same time on the way back. By then you'll be back in command.'

Kelso could see what Lew was saying. 'And if you're back in command, it'll be up to you to recommend what punishment we're given.'

'Do you realize what you're suggesting?' Hackett asked them as he let his gaze drift from man to man.

'We do, sir,' Shannon answered for them.

'And you're willing to lay your career on the line for Captain Kelso?'

'That's what he's doin' for *us*, major,' Shannon pointed out. 'If he's willin' to do that, then it's only fair that we be willin' to do the same for him.'

'You've changed your tune, sergeant.'

'Yes, sir,' Shannon replied. 'I've had cause to, sir.'

'Let's cut to it, major,' Kelso said impatiently. 'If you want my resignation when we return, you can have it. Hell, if you still want to court-martial me, then have at it. But don't allow Bragg to take the company out and kill all my men. Think about your daughter. We move fast, we move light and we can fight like hell. You *know* we're the only hope she has.'

After a pregnant pause, the Fort Whitethorn commander nodded. 'All right — do it. I'll deal with you, captain, when you return.'

It sounded ominous, but Kelso didn't care. With him leading, Company 'C' stood the best chance of accomplishing what was required.

'What about Bragg?' Kelso asked.

'I'll deal with him, too,' Hackett said with certainty.

Kelso knew of his ambitions for a political career, and that Bragg could provide the stepping-stone required to get there. He guessed that that ambition was about to fall away.

On the way out of the infirmary, Kelso said to Lew, 'Tell Seamus Murphy to come and see me. You come with him.'

Lew nodded and went to find the Irishman, while Kelso and Shannon were escorted back to the guardhouse.

★   ★   ★

'Do you see this, Barnes?' a voice said from outside the guardhouse. 'It's knocked out more men than you've had hot dinners. Now get the hell out of my way.'

'But the cap'n said no one goes in,' the guard protested.

'The cap'n ain't here, is he? Now let us in.'

The guard relented and let Murphy and Lew into Kelso's darkened cell.

The door was closed behind them and the three men settled down to discuss their next move.

'Did Lew tell you what's happening?' Kelso asked Murphy.

The Irishman nodded. 'He did.'

'I'm not going to order you to come with us, Seamus,' Kelso explained. 'But with Mordecai locked in here as well, I will need your help.'

'Mrs. Murphy's boy ain't missin' out on this for anythin', sor. You can count on me.'

'Thank you, Seamus, let's get to it.' Kelso went on to explain what he wanted. 'Have the men ready to go just after midnight. Have them discard any unnecessary equipment. Pack extra ammunition and we'll need some rope. Have them each carry an extra canteen. Did the new tomahawks get distributed?'

'Yes, sir.'

'All right — we'll be seeing you, then.'

'Just to clarify one thing, cap'n. You

want us to bust you and Mordecai out of here. Is that right?'

'Yes, it is. Do you have a problem with that?'

'Nope. But I was thinkin' that maybe Lew could get the men out while I'm settin' you and Shannon loose. Just in case some of the lads get a little trigger happy. You know how they are.'

'Good idea.'

'If that's all, sir, I'll start organizin' things.'

'Yes, that's all. But, if any of the men decide that they don't want to go against orders and ride with us, don't force them. I only want volunteers.'

'I'll take care of it.'

'Thanks, Seamus.'

* * *

The key rattled in the door around twenty minutes past midnight. It screeched open, the noise deafening in the stillness of the night. Murphy entered and said in a hushed voice,

'Let's go cap'n. The men are waitin' for us.'

'Good man.'

On the way out, Murphy released Shannon as well and they made their way outside. The fort was bathed in moonlight, the silvery glow casting long shadows across the parade ground. Turning to walk toward the main gate, Kelso almost bumped into a guard. He froze.

'It's all right, sir,' Murphy reassured him. 'Private Gleason is on our side.'

Kelso breathed out. 'Thank the Lord for that.'

The three men hurried around the perimeter of the parade ground, trying to keep to the shadows.

'How many men have we got, Seamus?' Kelso whispered.

'All of them, sor.'

'They *all* volunteered?'

'Yes, sor.'

'And you didn't have to . . . persuade them at all?'

'Not one whit, sor.'

164

A surge of pride rippled through Kelso as he followed behind the Irishman. Once outside the gates, they found the rest of Company 'C' waiting for them, alongside Lew. In addition, they found three spare horses, plus the weapons he and Shannon would need.

Kelso mounted up and looked across at Shannon. 'Let's get the hell out of here before they work out we're gone.'

With that, he led Company 'C' along the main street of Ocotillo Creek and set course for the Santa Rita Mountains.

★　★　★

'He's not there, sir. Neither of them are.'

Bragg looked up from what he'd been doing, a dumb expression on his face. 'What do you mean, not there?'

'They're gone. The whole of Company 'C' is gone.'

A slow burning rage flushed Bragg's face. He took a moment to compose himself before saying, 'Send Lieutenant Miller in to me.'

Thirty seconds later, Miller stood in front of Bragg. 'Did you hear?' asked Bragg.

'Yes, sir.'

'Then put a patrol together,' Bragg ordered. 'I'll lead it myself. Every damn one of them will be up on desertion charges.'

'Yes, sir.'

Miller snapped a sharp salute and spun on his heel. He disappeared out the door, leaving Bragg contemplating the pleasure of events to come. Outside, the brassy tones of assembly were already being sounded.

When it was all over, Bragg would finally be rid of Kelso, and he could form a new, and better, Company 'C'. And it would be all his to command.

Thirty minutes later, Bragg was outside on the parade ground, the twenty-man patrol he was to lead in pursuit of Kelso waiting patiently beside their horses.

'The men are ready, sir,' a pug-faced sergeant named Jones informed him. 'Just say the word.'

Eltham Jones was a forty-three-year-old soldier from Bragg's command, and he too had no love for Nathan Kelso or his men. He'd served in the Union cavalry, the 3rd Texas Brigade, during the War Between the States and was a career soldier.

'Get the men mounted, sergeant,' Bragg ordered.

'Just a moment, Captain Bragg.'

He turned to see Major Hackett approaching them. The major had to lean on a stick to help him walk, and struggled across the parade ground with Lieutenant Crispin Miller beside him. Hackett stopped in front of Bragg and Jones. In his hand, he held two pieces of paper.

'It's good to see you up and around, major,' Bragg said warily. 'We're about to go after Captain Kelso and his men.'

'You can forget about that, Captain Bragg,' Hackett snapped before turning his gaze on Jones. 'Sergeant, dismiss the men.'

Jones shot a questioning glance at Bragg, looking for a lead as to what he should do next.

'Sergeant!' Hackett snapped. 'Dismiss the men.'

'Ahh . . . yes, sir.'

'I don't mean to overstep, sir, but didn't you put me in charge of Fort Whitethorn?'

'I did,' Hackett acknowledged.

'Aren't I still in charge until you're well enough, and capable of resuming your duties?'

'That's correct.'

'In that case, we'll leave straight away and bring Kelso and his rabble in. Mount the men up, sergeant.'

'Sergeant, I told you to dismiss the men. Kindly do so,' Hackett countermanded.

'Sir.'

Bragg was dumbfounded. 'Sir, didn't you . . . ?'

Hackett held out the first of his

pieces of paper and gave it to the captain. 'It is a clearance from Doctor Sutton saying that I'm well enough to resume command of Fort Whitethorn. You are relieved, captain.'

'But — but . . . you can barely stand up! You can't be well enough to take over! You even look awful.'

Hackett sighed. 'You're right, captain. I'm starting to feel poorly again. I might have to return to the infirmary for a few more days.'

'It may well be for the best, sir,' Bragg nodded enthusiastically. 'Don't you worry, sir. I'll take care of everything.'

'No, there's no need, Captain Bragg,' Hackett held up the other piece of paper he had. 'This paper places Nathan Kelso in charge of Fort Whitethorn.'

Bragg was stunned. 'But . . . the man is a drunk!' he blustered. 'He broke out of the guardhouse.'

'He is the only officer out of the two of you who was not prepared to see his men massacred, and the women hostages placed in peril by a stupid, poorly planned attack,' Hackett hissed. 'Unlike you, who would have ridden them through the gates of hell just to curry favor with those higher up. Now get out of my sight, captain, before I bust you back to lieutenant!'

His face red, Bragg seethed. His eyes flicked to Miller and back to Hackett. 'I won't forget this, and I'm sure there are others that won't either.'

Hackett met his glare levelly. 'Dismiss, captain.'

Bragg opened his mouth to speak but instead, turned abruptly and stalked off. Hackett's shoulders sagged. The effort had taken a lot more from him than he'd expected. But at least now, Kelso would have a chance of getting his daughter back without interference from Dawson Bragg.

'We'll see how good your men are now,' he murmured before he turned and headed back to the infirmary, closely followed by his adjutant.

13

'I never asked how your leg was holding up, sergeant,' Kelso said, as they sat beside a small campfire, eating part of a desert bighorn sheep that Cass had managed to kill.

'It's fine, sir. A little stiff, but it's had time to mend.'

It had been a grueling day in the desert as they pushed their mounts hard to devour the distance. Having Cass along had been a blessing in disguise, for the Mescalero knew the locations of waterholes that even Lew Eden was unaware of. Kelso had asked him how he knew they were there, because Arizona wasn't traditionally part of Mescalero territory. The Apache had only shrugged his narrow shoulders and remained silent.

The yipping of a lonesome coyote drifted across the desert, carried a large distance on the clear night air. A couple of the men shifted nervously and peered out into the darkness as they remembered their recent experience with the rabid canines.

'How're the new men working out?'

'They'll be fine,' Shannon said confidently. 'They're good men.'

Kelso looked them over in the firelight. The Irishman, Michael Flannery, was a big man with red hair and a temper to match. He was a born soldier and seemed to fit in well. Willard Roberson was a rail-thin man with a rugged face. He was mostly quiet, but his excellent soldiering spoke for him.

That left Cass. Cassadore, the Mescalero Apache. He was wiry tough, wore a red bandanna headband and a blue cavalry shirt with the sleeves ripped from it. He also wore a breechcloth and high moccasins. His face was a deep walnut color, with dark eyes and high cheekbones. His hair was thick, long, and dark. So far, he had been worth his weight in gold.

'We'll rotate watches tonight and leave at dawn tomorrow,' Kelso said to Shannon.

'I'll see to it,' Shannon acknowledged.

Lew joined them and sat down to the left of Kelso.

'All quiet?' the captain asked.

'Nothin' stirrin' out there except for the coyotes, cap'n,' he reported. 'It's almost too quiet.'

Kelso nodded. 'Tomorrow I want Cass and you riding point together.'

'Sure thing,' Lew agreed.

'By my calculations, we should reach the Santa Ritas late in the afternoon. You agree?'

'Yup. Then it'll be another half a day until we reach the stronghold,' Lew told him.

'I might turn in, then, seeing as we have another long day tomorrow. Goodnight, gentlemen.'

★   ★   ★

173

The following day was much the same as the one before it — a hot, dusty ride through cactus and rock-strewn country. A barren waste where water was at a premium, but was found with ease by Cass. Mid-afternoon saw a change in scenery and temperature as they reached the Santa Ritas. They soon moved off the desert floor and into foothills covered with pine and oak scrub trees.

A few more hours on horseback saw them arrive in a narrow, steep-sided valley. They set up camp near a small stream where they could draw water. Unwilling to advertise their presence, Kelso gave orders for a cold camp, which meant there would be no fire.

His men were tired, but he knew they could handle whatever was thrown at them. When they reached the stronghold the following day, he planned to let them rest up until dark before they scaled the rock face. From there, they would wait until first light, then swoop down upon the Mimbreño camp.

Kelso was shaken awake sometime after midnight by Lew Eden.

'What is it?' he asked, still half asleep.

'We have a problem,' the scout informed him. 'We've been discovered.'

Now Kelso was wide-awake. This was the worst possible news he could've received. 'What? How?'

'A small group of Apaches must have cut our trail,' Lew explained. 'Cass discovered them scouting our camp. They're still out there. Four of them.'

Suddenly, as if on cue, the night erupted with gunfire.

'Damn it!' Kelso exclaimed, coming to his feet.

Somewhere in the darkness, he heard Shannon shout, 'Stand to!'

Kelso pulled his sidearm and hurried towards the sound of the gunshots. Bright flashes split the curtain of black, revealing moving shapes. Shouts grew louder and a scream of pain echoed throughout the camp.

As suddenly as it began, it was over. The sound of gunfire ceased but the echo slowly rolled away after bouncing from surrounding peaks. Out of the gloom, the familiar shape of Mordecai Shannon emerged.

'What the hell happened, sergeant?' Kelso asked testily.

'Indians, sir.'

'I know they were Indians, what I want to know is . . . ?'

Lew Eden appeared. 'One of the Apaches got away, cap'n.'

'Damn it,' Kelso cursed. 'Alright, take Ankrum and go after him. If we're not here when you return, you'll know where to find us.'

Lew disappeared and Kelso turned back to Shannon. 'Get the men mounted, Mordecai. We're leaving.'

Shannon hesitated.

'What?' Kelso asked.

'Private Dickerson was wounded,' Shannon said.

'Bad?'

'He's dead,' Lane Carr informed them as he emerged from the inky blackness. 'He didn't last long. Shot through the chest.'

'Any others?' inquired Kelso.

'Nope, just him.'

They'd been lucky. With all that lead flying around, there could have been more than just one casualty. But it was cold comfort just about then.

'All right. Get Dickerson buried and then we'll move out of here.'

'Sir.'

Turning back to Shannon, he ordered, 'I want Cass out on point. Tell him if anything moves out there I want to know about it.'

'Yes, sor.'

Shannon disappeared, leaving Kelso standing by himself. This was all they needed. If the remaining Apache escaped, it would all be over before it even began.

★ ★ ★

Lew drew the paint to a halt. He dropped his hand so that it rested upon his revolver. Ankrum reined in beside him and with a confused expression on his face, asked, 'Why've we stopped?'

'He's here,' Lew said.

'What?'

'The Apache. He's stopped running. He's here.'

'Where?'

Lew shrugged. 'Somewhere ahead.'

'How can you tell?'

Suddenly a startled bird took flight, its wings beating furiously as it weaved through the trees.

'Get off the trail!' Lew yelled, kicking the paint hard in the flanks.

A *fizz* sounded and was followed by a dull *thunk!* An arrow sprouted from Ankrum's barrel chest. The big man looked down at it, his eyes wide with surprise.

'Hey Lew, he's killed me.'

He looked around for the scout, but Lew was nowhere to be seen. Silently, Ankrum slid sideways from the saddle and landed on the rough trail in an untidy heap. He twitched once and then lay still.

Lew's horse had moved into the trees in a couple of bounds, and there the scout leaped from the saddle, taking shelter behind a clump of rocks. From his crouched position, he saw Ankrum fall and cursed under his breath. Another Company 'C' original was gone.

Swiftly, the scout circled to his left until he found a deadfall with scattered clumps of brush around it. He knelt down and waited for what seemed like an age. Nothing moved at first. The landscape was silent. Not even the birds chirped.

Then something moved on the other side of the trail. It wasn't anything obvious, just a small flicker. Lew's eyes locked onto the spot and he waited. It didn't take long for a head full of long black hair, tied back by a rawhide thong, to appear.

The Indian moved parallel with the trail in smooth, silent movements. He was wraithlike, as though his moccasins never touched the uneven ground.

Lew tucked his pistol into his belt

and drew his hatchet. Stealth was the key here, to kill the Apache as silently as possible so no gunshots would be heard and raise the alarm.

He waited for the Apache to pass, then padded across the trail and slipped into the brush on the other side. He then started to follow him as quietly as he could.

He crouched down beside a yucca that grew up next to a large rock. He waited and listened for a telltale sign that would give the Apache's position away. Once more, nothing stirred. Minutes dragged by and the surrounding brush and forest remained quiet.

It was a waiting game in which both men were determined not to be the loser. To lose was to die. But waiting here wasn't getting it done either and, against his better judgment, Lew moved to follow the Mimbreño.

He'd gone no more than three steps when a whisper of movement to his left made him swivel around. As he did, the hatchet in his right hand swept across his body in a swift strike.

The Mimbreño's rock-hard body slammed into him and knocked him flat. The hatchet's lightning-fast blow had scored a deep cut along the Apache's ribs, but failed to cause a fatal injury. Blood flowed freely from the wound, soaking Lew's shirt as he wrestled with the attacker on top of him.

The Apache's snarl was animal-like as he desperately tried to kill the scout. He held a knife in his right fist and tried to bring it down in a rapid movement directed at Lew's throat. The point was only an instant from killing Lew when he managed to grab the Apache's wrist in his own ham-sized left hand.

Lew squeezed his opponent's hand tight until he felt the bones in the Apache's wrist grind together. The snarling Indian gasped as pain shot up his arm and into his shoulder. The scout twisted the wrist and he felt the bones finally give. The Indian's hand opened reflexively. An animalistic howl was emitted by the Indian as he dropped the knife.

Once more, the stone-headed hatchet swept up. This time, its finely honed blade buried deep into the juncture of the Apache's shoulder and neck. Blood spurted and the Indian stiffened. Lew wrenched the hatchet free and swung it hard. The savage blow sliced into the side of the Apache's throat, severing his jugular.

Great gouts of blood pulsed from the gaping wound. The Apache reached up to try to stem the flow of his life source, but it was no use. He was dead within seconds.

The scout rolled him off and climbed to his feet. He drew in large gulps of air and looked down at the dead Indian. The Apache's eyes were wide and sightless as they stared up at the sky. Lew placed the hatchet back into its sheath. Turning, he walked over to where Ankrum lay. As he'd thought, the soldier was dead.

He looked about and sighted the dead man's horse. He caught it up, then loaded Ankrum across the saddle. Then he climbed aboard the paint and rode off to find the rest of Company 'C'.

14

'Two men dead already, and we've not reached our destination yet,' Kelso said solemnly.

He wanted a drink.

'It's the nature of the beast, sir,' Shannon said. 'Every man here knows it could happen whenever they go out.'

'I know,' Kelso acknowledged. 'But knowing it doesn't make it any better. You'd best see him buried Mordecai.'

'Sir.'

'How far to go from here, Lew?' Kelso asked, looking around the surrounding ridges strewn with rocks and pines.

'A few more hours.'

'All right. Find Cass, he's out on point somewhere. I've not seen him all morning, so there's either no trouble ahead, or he's dead.'

'I doubt he's dead,' Lew murmured.

'Well, when you find him, you need to make him understand that when he doesn't report back, I'm just as blind as if he wasn't here,' Kelso snapped testily.

'I'll make sure he understands.'

Lew turned to walk away, then paused. He reached inside his coat and pulled out a dirt-stained envelope. 'You might want this, Nathan. I took it from Ankrum. It is a letter from his sister. I thought you might want to write her about . . . you know. It has an address on it.'

Kelso nodded and reached for it. His hand trembled violently and he needed two passes at the envelope before he managed to grasp it.

'Thanks,' he said, frustration evident in his voice.

Lew scowled. 'You all right?'

'I'm fine,' Kelso snapped.

He watched Lew walk away, then looked down at his hands. The trembling was still there. He concentrated, trying to stop them by will

185

alone. The tremors only got worse. Finally, frustrated, he flexed them a couple of times and dropped them to his side. Damn it!

Once Ankrum had been laid to rest, Kelso, along with the rest of Company 'C', mounted their horses and made the final push on toward the Apache stronghold. When they reached their destination, Lew had them halt in a stand of pines. He pointed at the sloped rock face in front of them. 'That's it.'

Kelso stared at the three hundred feet of granite before him. It seemed to just go up and not stop. Shaking his head, he asked, 'You *climbed* that?'

'In the daylight,' Lew reminded him. 'Not in the dark.'

For the first time, Kelso had doubts. Not about his men, more for what they were expected to do. 'When you said we had to climb, I had no idea it'd be something like this.'

'I'll go up before dark,' Lew informed him. 'I'll take the rope we brought, and once I'm at the top, I'll tie it off. The rest can use it in the dark. That will make things a little easier.'

'Not ideal, but I guess it's better than nothing,' Kelso allowed. 'I'll see you before you go.'

'I'll get ready.'

Shannon and Seamus Murphy sought him out next.

'Cap'n, we were just talkin',' Shannon said, 'and we got to thinkin' that maybe we need somebody guardin' the front door to this place, just in case we need 'em.'

'Might be an idea,' Kelso agreed. 'Do you have anyone in mind?'

'Myself and two others,' Murphy said. 'Napier and Roberson.'

'All right, do it. Be in position by morning. Once the sun starts to come up, we'll attack.'

'Yes, sor.'

Murphy left them to it and went to find the men he required for their particular task. Shannon looked up the rock face and wondered what it would be like.

'Out with it, Mordecai. Tell me I'm crazy.'

'If you are sir, then I am too. After all, I'll be climbin' up there in the dark right alongside you.'

'Once we get to the top, I want to make sure the women are going to be safe when we attack,' Kelso explained. 'I'm going to send Lew and Cass into the Apache camp to watch over them.'

'That's mighty risky, sir,' Shannon said warily.

'Yes, it probably is, but it's got to be done,' Kelso told him firmly. 'They're the reason we're here. If we lose even one of them, I'll consider this mission a failure.'

'Well, we'd best keep them all alive,' Shannon said. 'But if it's all the same to you, I'd like to be one of those to go into camp.'

Kelso shook his head. 'Out of the question. If something happens to me, you're the one the men'll look to to get them through. You can't do that from the middle of the Apache camp.'

Shannon nodded. He knew Kelso was right.

'Do you want to leave a man with the horses?'

'No, we don't have anyone to spare.'

'All right. Then I guess all we have to do now is wait for dark.'

'And then God give us strength,' Kelso murmured.

* * *

Kelso's foot slipped from the rock lip and he flailed, about looking for purchase, his mind trying to block all thoughts of falling. Coarse rope bit into his left hand and he choked back a cry, his heart pounding wildly.

'Are you all right, sir?' Brady whispered from below him.

Gathering himself, Kelso whispered back, 'Yes. Keep climbing.'

God only knew how far they'd come. All Kelso knew was that the muscles in his arms burned and his legs felt like jelly. Sweat ran down his face and stung his eyes, even though the night was cool. He reached up with his right hand and grasped the rope, hauling himself up a little more.

He chanced a look up. The man in front of him, Carr, was now only a dark shape. He cursed himself inwardly for being so slow.

Inch after pain-filled inch, minute by minute, Kelso dragged himself up the rope until he felt rough hands grasp him by his shirt and drag him over the edge at the top.

'Take it easy,' Lew whispered. 'We got you.'

Kelso crawled out of the way and lay on his back, his lungs sucking in deep breaths. Relief flooded through him, knowing that the hardest part was over. The burning sensation in his extremities slowly ebbed and he sat up.

'Sergeant Shannon?'

There was movement beside him and a familiar voice said, 'Here, sir.'

'How many more are left to come up?'

'Five, sir.'

Kelso nodded. 'We'll rest here for a while, then move off. I want total silence when we do.'

'I'll see to it.'

'Good. When Lew has a moment, tell him I'd like to see him.'

'Sir.'

Five minutes later, Lew appeared out of the dark. 'You wanted me, cap'n?'

'Do you think that you and Cass could sneak into the Apache camp and secure the women until we attack?'

There was a drawn-out silence as the scout thought hard about the proposal.

'It's your choice, Lew. If you say it can't be done, then we'll go with what we've got.'

'We can do it,' Lew finally decided.

'Good. Work it so you're not hanging out there too long before we attack.'

'We'll go in about an hour before. It'll give us time if the goin' is slow.'

'Got it. Good luck.'

'Just don't forget where we are. I'd hate to be shot by one of our own.'

Kelso smiled. 'Just in case, you'd better keep your head down.'

Eden and Cass moved like wraiths through the blackened surrounds of the Mimbreño stronghold. Because the wickiup holding the women was on the far side of the Apache camp, they had to navigate their way cautiously until they were in position. The absence of outlying sentries made things considerably easier.

Both men crouched by a large rock as they surveyed the camp. A dull light cast from the low burning central campfire showed some of the prone figures as they slept. The enormity of their task hit Lew suddenly and a prickle of doubt entered his mind. There were upwards of thirty Apaches scattered about the stronghold, and the attacking force was only one-third that size. Surprise was essential for them to succeed.

Lew made to move forward when Cass's hand shot out and grasped his arm. He quickly took a knee and glanced at the Mescalero scout, who used his chin to point at the camp.

A tall Mimbreño had stood up from his sleeping position and was walking toward them. He weaved his way between other sleeping forms until he was no more than twenty feet from the two observers. The Apache then proceeded to relieve himself near a small shrub before returning to his resting place.

Lew let out the breath he'd been holding. He patted Cass' hand as a gesture of thanks, then made to move toward the wickiup once more.

He'd gone no more than two steps when the darkness produced another Mimbreño. The Apache froze when he saw Lew standing before him, trying to comprehend what was happening. His mouth opened to shout a warning to the rest of the sleeping Apaches.

Lew's right arm blurred in a

desperate movement. At the center of the arc, his hand released the stone-headed hatchet and it flew true. The honed blade embedded into the half-naked Apache's chest with an audible, hollow *thunk!*

Lew was hoping the Apache would die silently.

He didn't.

A high-pitched scream escaped him, sounding unbelievably loud in the early morning quiet.

Lew leaped forward, grasped the hatchet's handle and wrenched it from the prone Apache's form. He brought it down again across the throat, cutting the scream short, but it was too little, too late. Already the camp was boiling to life.

And then all hell broke loose.

15

It was at that moment that Kelso's fears came true. A scream filled the air, followed by a furious eruption of gunfire.

Hidden out of sight above the stronghold, Company 'C' came alive as they waited for orders from their commander.

'God damn it!' Kelso hissed. 'Sergeant Shannon!'

Shannon appeared by his side. 'Sir?'

'Take half the men and hit them on the right flank, I'll take the rest and hit them on the left. Go in hard. Tomahawks and pistols. If we catch them from both sides, we might still be in with a show. But they need to be mindful of the women!'

'Yes, sir.'

Shannon picked some men and disappeared into the gloom. Kelso ran over to Baranski. 'Benny. You and the others follow me.'

Without waiting to see if they were following, Kelso took off at a run. He weaved between rocks and ducked under tree limbs as he traversed the uneven ground. Finally, when they were in position, he raised his right hand. In it was his army issue Colt.

He took a deep breath and shouted, '*Charge!*'

They ran forward into the maelstrom.

* * *

When the gunfire started, a hail of bullets and arrows buzzed all around Lew and Cass. The Mescalero cried out when a bullet struck his upper thigh. He fell to the ground beside Lew, while the scout pulled his pistol and began to return fire.

A slug tore at his shirt, opened the material but left no mark on his skin. The next one burned his left bicep near his shoulder, while a third nicked a shallow furrow in the flesh on his right side.

Lew gritted his teeth at the searing pain and dropped to his knees behind a rock. Bullets peppered the boulder and chips flew through the air. There was a moan of pain from beside him and he remembered Cass.

'You okay?' he called out above the melee.

'I live,' Cass shouted back. 'Hit in leg.'

Another flurry of gunfire whipped around their position.

'Can you get up?'

'No.'

'All right. Hang on. Keep shootin'.'

There was only one thing for it, Lew decided. The wickiup. They needed to reach it and wait there for help from Kelso. He gritted his teeth in preparation for lifting his companion, bent down and grabbed Cass by the collar of his shirt with his left hand.

As he did, a menacing shape loomed

out of the darkness. With his pistol in his right hand, Lew squeezed the trigger. The gun spat flame as it bucked in his hand and the impact of the bullet stopped the oncoming Apache in his tracks. He stiffened and fell to the ground.

'Hang on, Cass, this is goin' to hurt,' Eden barked, and commenced half-carrying, half-dragging the wounded man towards the wickiup. When he reached the rough stick wall of the shelter, he hauled Cass through the entry and turned around to speak to the women with the hope of easing their anxieties.

Instead, he whispered, 'Oh, no.'

They were too late.

$\star \quad \star \quad \star$

Shannon fired two shots and the big Mimbreño fell to the ground, his face shot away. Another came at him with a knife and the sergeant buried his tomahawk in his middle. The Apache doubled over and Shannon placed the barrel of the gun against his head and squeezed the trigger.

The Apache's head was blown apart and he fell, but Shannon was swift, and tore the tomahawk free, already preparing for the next round.

More shapes loomed in front of the advancing soldiers. A pained shout from beside Shannon pulled his attention from the new threat. A quick glance to his left revealed another of his number going down. It was Brady, the Texan.

'You all right?' Shannon shouted above the bedlam.

Before he could answer, an Apache emerged from the dark, swinging an old Spencer carbine like a club. Brady managed to raise his sidearm and fire a shot that punched into the Indian's middle.

'Gotcha, you son of a bitch,' he cursed loudly, then fell onto his side.

'Damn it!' Shannon swore, as four more Apaches advanced on him from out of the darkness.

He raised his six-gun to fire but the hammer fell on an empty chamber.

* * *

The Mimbreño blindsided Kelso, slamming his tough wiry body into the white-eye, knocking him flat. The air whooshed from Kelso's lungs and the Apache, having finished on top of him, raised a large knife to deliver a brutal deathblow to the stunned captain.

Kelso's eyes grew wide at the realization that he would be unable to prevent it. Then the Indian's head snapped sideways unexpectedly, blood and gore splashing over Kelso's uniform. The report of the shot seemed far off, and it wasn't until the large form of Baranski filled his vision, that Kelso knew what had happened.

The Cossack leaned down and grabbed Kelso by the shirt, hauling him to his feet.

'No time for rest,' Baranski said in a

terse voice. 'Stay on feet.'

A slug struck the big Ukrainian in the left shoulder, the sound audible above the din of battle. He lurched noticeably and dropped his six-gun, but managed to stay on his feet.

'*Ublyudok!*' he snarled. 'Bastard!'

And then the bearded giant raised the tomahawk in his right hand and stalked off to continue the fight.

Around him, Kelso saw his men engaged in vicious combat and hoped that some of them, at least, would survive. Deep down, though, he had a nagging sense that this could be Company 'C's last hurrah.

★　★　★

'Somethin's wrong, Sarge,' Napier said, his concern evident. 'We gotta get up there and help 'em.'

Murphy knew he was right. He shared the same concerns. The gunfire had erupted too early. It wasn't meant to happen until dawn. Now the stronghold was engulfed in a full-scale firefight and an extra three men might make all the difference.

They had hidden the horses a short distance away in the trees and now lay concealed, listening to the ebb and flow of the shooting.

'Roberson, get the horses and break your damned bugle out,' the Irishman decided. 'We're goin' up.'

* * *

Shannon had resigned himself to death and was expecting it when Flannery came charging past him shouting a stream of obscenities. The Irishman threw himself into the midst of the approaching Mimbreños, flailing left and right with tomahawk and pistol.

Two of the four fell under his devastating blows, while the others kept coming. Taking up his own tomahawk, Shannon came to his feet and leaped into the throng of battle, helping Flannery overcome the final two Apaches.

Breathing heavily from his exertions, Shannon said, 'Thanks for that, I was dead for sure if you hadn't come along.'

The Irishman turned to face Shannon, his movements jerky. 'I kinda wish I hadn't.'

Flannery fell forward into the sergeant's arms. Shannon heard the death rattle as the Irishman breathed his last.

Shannon was twisted inside by a terrible kind of anguish. 'Damn it, Irish,' he said, 'what did you go and do that for?'

He eased the dead man to the ground and quickly reloaded.

'Sergeant Shannon, are you all right?' Lane Carr shouted from beside him.

'Yes, keep goin'.'

'Where?'

Shannon looked around. 'The wickiup. Head for the wickiup. I'll follow you.'

When they reached their destination, they got the same shock Lew Eden had.

Their sudden appearance caused Lew to raise his gun but he quickly recognized them and put the gun up.

'Good way to get yourself shot,' he rumbled.

'A bullet might be a quicker way to go than if them Mimbreños get their hands on us,' Shannon allowed. 'Where are the women?'

'Not here,' Lew answered.

'Damn it.'

'Carr, take a look at Cass, he's wounded,' Lew said. And to Shannon: 'I found something else here instead.'

'What?'

'A crate of Winchester rifles.'

'That means the slavers have got 'em,' Shannon muttered.

'Yeah.'

'Any ammunition for the Winchesters?'

'I should imagine so.'

'Then let's get 'em workin', Lew. Finally, we might just stand a chance.'

⋆　⋆　⋆

The morning dawned iron gray with an overcast sky. Kelso's face was painted red, a fresh cut above his left eye bleeding freely. For the second time in as many minutes, his revolver's hammer clicked on a dead cartridge. Beside him, Baranski and Fitch fought desperately to stay alive. Both bore the bloodstains of wounds received in the fight for survival.

'I'm out of ammunition!' Kelso shouted.

'Me too!' Fitch shouted back.

Baranski stepped forward in true Cossack style and stated defiantly, 'Then we die with honor.'

Kelso held up his tomahawk and stepped in beside the snarling Ukrainian. Faced with certain death, he felt a sudden release, as though a weight had been lifted from his shoulders. Even the shakes were gone. A crazy smile split his face as he said to Baranski, 'I'll race you to hell, Benny.'

'Pah,' the big man snorted. 'Follow me, I show you the way.'

Both men started to run towards the center of the stronghold, where a number of Mimbreños had concentrated.

'Wait for me!' Fitch shouted after them. 'You ain't havin' all the fun!'

Into the throng they charged, their impact crushing. Hammer blows fell and Apaches went down in bloody heaps. Kelso knew, however, that once the initial shock of their surprise attack wore off, it wouldn't take long for the Apaches to gain the upper hand, and it would be all over.

From of the corner of his eye, he noticed Baranski stagger from a stunning blow to his head by a rifle butt. The big Cossack went down on one knee, holding his good arm above his head to ward off the next blow.

It never came, because right then the brassy tones of a bugle blowing the charge rang out across the stronghold and changed the complexion of the battle.

The Mimbreños just seemed to melt away. One moment they were all over the men of Company 'C' and the next, they were gone and the sounds of battle died away.

Standing in the cold gray light of dawn with a bloody tomahawk in his fist, Kelso was confused at how they could just disappear.

The eerie silence was replaced by the sound of hoofs as the three horsemen thundered into the Apache camp.

'Where did they go?' Kelso asked. 'They just disappeared.'

'They do that, when they don't care much for the odds,' said Seamus Murphy, riding up.

Kelso turned to look at the sergeant, his face frozen in a stunned expression. 'Thanks, Seamus.'

'What do you want me to do?' Murphy asked.

'Check on the rest of the men,' Kelso told him. 'See who's still left. I'll check on the women.'

As he closed on the wickiup, he saw Lew and Shannon standing in front of it. 'I'm glad to see you both still alive.'

'It was a close thing all around,'

Shannon allowed. 'If it wasn't for the bugle, we'd all be worm food by now. They must've thought there was a whole other company comin' after them.'

'Where're the women?' Kelso asked.

It was Lew who told him. 'They're not here.'

'We found these in their place,' Shannon said, tossing the brand-new Winchester in his hands across to Kelso.

Kelso stared at the weapon, stunned. They were too late to save the women, and the action had cost him who knows how many dead and wounded.

'How many of these were there?'

'However many's in the crate inside the wickiup,' Shannon said.

Kelso looked it over. It was a '76 model chambered for a .45-.75 round. He tossed it back to Shannon. 'If there are enough, issue one to each of the men and destroy the rest. Company 'C' might as well have some decent rifles.'

Shannon nodded, 'Yes, sir.'

Next, Kelso looked at Lew. 'I've got another job for you.'

'I figured you might.'

'We have to find out where the women have gone. Can you and Cass get onto it?'

'I can,' Eden acknowledged. 'Cass can't. He was wounded.'

'Bad?'

'He'll live.'

'All right. You'll have to go it alone, then.'

'I'll get right on it.'

Kelso was left standing alone, and as he gazed around, he wondered if there were sufficient able-bodied men to finish the job.

16

'We got two dead and another four wounded,' Shannon reported fifteen minutes later.

Kelso nodded grimly. 'Who?'

'Flannery and Teeters were killed, and Brady, Baranski, Cass, and McGee were wounded. Some others, includin' yourself by the looks of it, have minor wounds.'

'Will they all make it?'

'The only one Carr is concerned about is Brady.'

Kelso nodded. 'Detail Murphy to get the wounded back to Whitethorn,' Kelso ordered. 'You and I, along with Lew Eden, will go after the slavers and get the women back.'

'I'll see to it, sir.'

Kelso went looking for Carr and found him hovering over Brady. The Texan looked to be in a bad way. He was unconscious and the Company 'C' medic was taking the opportunity to clean up his wound as best he could.

'How's he doing?'

'He's not good, sir,' Carr said, looking up. 'He took a bullet in the right side of his chest. I've managed to stop the bleeding, but I've no idea what kind of damage it's done to his innards.'

'Did you manage to get the bullet out?'

'Yes, sir. It was made easier by him bein' out to it.'

'What about the other wounded? Can they make it back to Whitethorn?'

'They should be fine.'

'Good. I've detailed Seamus to take you all back,' he explained. 'Myself, Sergeant Shannon, and Lew Eden are going after the women.'

'Do you want me along?'

Kelso looked at Brady and shook his head. 'No. You've got your hands full with him. Just do what you can and we'll see you back at the fort.'

'Sir.'

It took almost two hours before they were ready to transport the wounded back to Whitethorn. During that time, they buried Flannery and Teeters, and Roberson played Taps over the graves once they were finished.

The wounded Apaches were treated by Carr. There were only two. However, the Mimbreños had suffered fifteen dead. Kelso made the decision not to bury them, but leave them where they lay, anticipating that the others would return to reclaim them.

By the time Murphy was ready to leave, Lew had returned. He'd found a wagon trail left by the slavers, which was a good place for them to start.

'All right,' Kelso said grimly. 'Let's *finish* this.'

★　★　★

The desert air crackled with great forks of electric-blue lightning, and the relative peace was shattered by the crash of thunder that followed almost immediately. The deep gray clouds smothered the sun, preventing any rays from getting through. To the west, a great curtain of rain approached, blanketing everything in that direction with life-giving water. Another flash was followed soon after by a ground-shaking boom. The wind picked up suddenly, and the three men who lay belly-down on the low rock and cactus-strewn ridge, knew that the rain would soon reach them.

The trail had led them out of the Santa Rita Mountains and back onto the desert to the east. For two days they'd tracked the wagon, losing its trail twice then finding it again, eventually bringing them to where they were now.

'Is that what I think it is?' Kelso asked.

'Looks to me to be an old tumbleweed wagon that the marshals used to transport prisoners in the Nations,' Lew replied.

'I can see the women,' Shannon said, passing Kelso's field glasses back to him. 'Down there near the wagon, you'll see a large saguaro. To the left of that, there's a clump of rocks, and that's where they are.'

Kelso brought the field glasses up to his eyes just as another flare of lightning split the sky above them. He flinched involuntarily when the thunder came, then panned left and right until he found the prisoners. Shannon had been right. They were huddled together near the clump of rocks. They looked reasonably well, but Kelso wouldn't know that for sure until they were freed.

He moved the glasses right and found five slavers sitting around a campfire drinking coffee.

'That's a bit careless of them,' Kelso said aloud.

'What's that, cap'n?' asked Lew.

'They don't have any pickets out.'

'Bad for them, good for us,' Shannon grated.

Further investigation revealed their horses tied close to the wagon, and a shallow dry wash that ran along the rear of the campsite. He passed the glasses back to Shannon.

'Mordecai, can you make out the dry wash behind their camp?'

'Yes, sir.'

'Use that for cover to get in behind them,' Kelso told him. 'Lew and I will come in from different directions and we'll have them out-positioned. We need to get it done before it gets too dark.'

'Give me twenty minutes and I'll be ready,' Shannon said and slipped away, carrying one of the newly acquired Winchesters.

'Whatever happens, Lew, we get the women back.'

'Keep your head down, cap'n,' Lew replied and moved away to get into position. Just then, the rain started to come down in sheets.

* * *

Rain ran in rivulets from Kelso's hat brim as he eased his way past the

215

wagon and around the corner of the rocks. It was almost dark now with the rain and heavy cloud combination, so he knew they would have to act soon.

The moment he moved into view of the rain-soaked women huddled together, the one closest to him opened her mouth to scream.

Kelso held a finger to his lips to try and stop her, but the woman was clearly traumatized and had gone beyond the point of no return. It was only due to quick thinking by one of the other women, who clamped her hand over the woman's mouth, that the scream was silenced.

'My name is Captain Nathan Kelso,' he whispered hurriedly. 'I'm from Fort Whitethorn.'

He heard one of them gasp and he turned his gaze to the young lady in the stained light-blue dress.

'Amelia Hackett?' he guessed.

She nodded.

Kelso smiled at her and said to them all, 'Stay here and don't move.'

Standing up, Kelso called out and walked forward.

'Hello the camp,' he called through the curtain of rain.

Lightning flashed overhead and brightened the surrounding landscape enough for Kelso to see the gun coming up in his direction.

The Winchester in his hands whip-lashed and the report died amid the crash of thunder that rolled across the desert. Kelso saw the muzzle flash from the gun the slaver had brought up and felt the slug pass close to his head. He fired again and this time the slaver fell.

Gunshots blended with the thunder of the storm and in the blue-tinged flashes of lightning, the slavers performed a macabre dance of death. Their bodies jerked as bullets drove into them from three different directions. It was brief and violent and when it was over, every one of the slavers lay dead in the mud. The pools of water forming around their bodies turned red as their blood seeped out.

Kelso levered a fresh round into the chamber of the Winchester and walked forward. He was joined by Shannon and Eden, who appeared out of the darkening gloom. They stared down briefly at the dead men in silence before Kelso said, 'Let's get the women and go home.'

★   ★   ★

'Major, they're coming in,' Crispin Miller announced, as he threw open the door so hard it banged against the wall. 'Sorry, sir. Captain Kelso's back. They're coming through the gates now!'

It had been five days since Seamus Murphy and the wounded had returned with news of the mission to rescue Hackett's daughter and the other women. His despair had returned when Murphy informed him that his daughter, along with the others, had already been sold to slavers for a crate of Winchesters.

Now, Hackett struggled to his feet and crossed the room to look out the window. The bright sunlight made his head hurt, and Hackett blinked several times to clear his vision. He frowned as he watched them stop on the parade ground. Kelso was out front on his horse, alongside Lew Eden. Mordecai Shannon sat atop some sort of wagon. It appeared to be a prisoner conveyance and Shannon was in the driver's seat. They all climbed down and walked around to the back of it. Kelso opened the door and the women slowly climbed out.

As soon as he saw Amelia, Hackett made a sound deep in his throat and hurried outside. He met her on a dusty section of the parade ground where they embraced fiercely, unwilling to let one another go, just in case. When they finally parted, Amelia was ushered inside by one of the married women, while the others were subjected to the same treatment by another woman. When his daughter was out of sight,

Hackett turned to face the three men who stood waiting nearby. His eyes, glistening fiercely, went directly to Kelso.

'Thank you, captain,' he said gratefully. 'I hear you've had a tough time of it?'

Kelso's shoulders slumped. He was bone tired and it showed in his reply. 'Yes, sir. But we did what we set out to do.'

'For that, I'm truly thankful,' Hackett allowed. His eyes shifted to Shannon and Lew. 'Thankful to all of you . . . and to the men of Company 'C'.'

There was an awkward silence between them which Kelso broke by saying, 'If you don't mind, major, I'd like to get cleaned up and see my company.'

'Yes, certainly,' Hackett acknowledged. 'You'll be happy to know that your man, Brady came through all right.'

A surge of relief flowed through Kelso at the news. 'Thank you, sir.'

'Quite. Maybe a little later, you and your men could join me for a drink?' Hackett suggested.

Kelso could feel the eyes of Lew and Shannon on him. A drink sounded real good about then. But he shook his head and said, 'That's a generous offer, sir but I'll have to decline.'

Hackett's expression showed his approval. 'As you wish. The offer is still good later if you change your mind.'

'Thank you, sir . . . but I won't.'

Shannon cleared his throat meaningfully.

'Yes, sergeant?' Hackett asked.

'If it's all the same to you, major, we'd be interested in joinin' you.'

'By all means, sergeant. You and Mr. Eden are most welcome.'

Hackett turned and left, leaving Kelso standing with Shannon and Eden. 'You men may as well go and get cleaned up. Otherwise, you'll be late.'

'I know we lost some good men this time out, sir,' Shannon said, 'but don't hold it against yourself. For what it's worth, you did some good soldierin' out there, and if I had to choose, I'd choose you.'

'Thank you, Mordecai. Dismiss.'

Kelso's gaze drifted to Lew. The scout gave him an almost imperceptible nod before he turned away and left Kelso all alone.

Shannon was right. They had lost some very good men, but they were sure to lose more. While the Apaches continued to raid this side of the border, it was inevitable.

He looked down at his hands.

The shakes had returned.